HERE
COMES
THE
DREAMER

HERE
COMES
THE
DREAMER

a novella
Carole Giangrande

inanna poetry & fiction series

INANNA PUBLICATIONS AND EDUCATION INC.
TORONTO, CANADA

We gratefully acknowledge the support of the Canada Council for the Arts and the Ontario Arts Council for our publishing program. We also acknowledge the financial support of the Government of Canada through the Canada Book Fund

Cover design: Val Fullard

Library and Archives Canada Cataloguing in Publication

Giangrande, Carole, 1945–, author
        Here comes the dreamer : a novella / by Carole Giangrande.

(Inanna poetry & fiction series)
Issued in print and electronic formats.
ISBN 978-1-77133-250-7 (paperback). — ISBN 978-1-77133-249-1 (epub).
— ISBN 978-1-77133-252-1 (pdf)

        I. Title. II. Series: Inanna poetry and fiction series

PS8563.I24H47 2015   C813'.54   C2015-904991-1
                                               C2015-904992-X

Printed and bound in Canada

Inanna Publications and Education Inc.
210 Founders College, York University
4700 Keele Street, Toronto, Ontario, Canada M3J 1P3
Telephone: (416) 736-5356 Fax: (416) 736-5765
Email: inanna.publications@inanna.ca   Website: www.inanna.ca

For my family

O Moon, O Bitter Earth

1

TROUBLE CAME TO ALASTAIR LUCE like a nasty slap of a wave at high tide, one wave after another. He'd been happy at times, but happiness was a breaker and it crashed and broke on the hard rock of the unexpected. Sorrow was no different. He wondered if it had been his fate to live by water so that he would cling to nothing at all.

Yet he didn't love the sea and its moodiness. He'd worked as a house painter, and he'd brought to this meticulous task his care for all that was solid and enduring. From high on his ladder, he'd view the street where he and Nora had once lived, and he'd imagine its rooftops and turrets, newel posts and cornices painted in the brilliance of his inner seeing, of his vivid dreams at night. It never troubled him that he'd had to paint in the modest hues that his customers preferred. It made no difference. Colour smouldered inside his fingers and he could feel the force of it, electric under the stillness of everything he touched. A patient man, he knew that this extraordinary power would bide its time as a shoot did in a humble bulb, waiting for sunlight to prod it into bloom. On his canvases at home, he'd try to paint the ineffable light that hovered under the surface of his life. He'd drink, but only when his suffering became too great, his sorrow that he couldn't capture much of anything.

Which was why trouble came, he told himself years later.

Yet his hope was as tough as a weed in rock, as mindless as a fist in a bully's face. He'd come to feel that hope was part of the packaging of skin and muscle, nerve and bone, a thing you strengthened as you bore the weight of living. This was why he'd shown up for Lyle Miller's funeral. He'd hoped to see his own daughter, longing to assure her that nothing lasts, including grief.

"You're my dad, not him," said Grace when he'd called. She hadn't asked about Nora.

"If you come, we'll have a chance to talk," he'd said.

"I'll come," she'd answered.

Alastair forgave her, that she lived outside the constraints of time. Her *I'll come* was about as punctual as a tiny stream finding its way to the sea. He could peer through Grace and see cities rising along the banks of her mind, long-hidden streets where she'd wandered since childhood. He hoped she'd forgiven him the years when they might have been closer to each other. Seventy-eight years old he was, and time was no longer his friend. Neither was the man who'd died.

Gracie, how I wish you'd come, but he understood. How many miles was Toronto from here? Five hundred or so? Grace couldn't drive, wouldn't fly.

Had she come, she'd be seated next to Nora in the front row, but he was imagining his own death, as if he and Nora and Grace were still a family, and they were mourning him. It had been a while since he'd seen his former wife, ill herself with a bad heart, and he noticed that Nora's warm-ember hair had become a snowdrift. How thin she was, her gentle plumpness gone, as if in the anguish of Lyle's dying, each passing day had carved off some of the meat of her life, trimming it away from the solid bone of her marriage. Years ago, he'd suffered these same wounds when she left him.

Thirteen years he'd spent with Nora.

Lyle Miller leaves his wife of forty years, said the obit. *His children, Grace and John*. Alastair had pulled the single page from the paper, bunched it up and thrown it in the garbage. With it went a residue of bitterness, and in its place, he felt grief and a stirring of compassion. He couldn't watch sorrow crush Nora as it had done with him. How grateful he was for a heart that spoke before his lips could mutter *serves you right*. *Nora, I know how you feel, I know.*

Behind Nora sat Claire Bernard, married to Lyle's nephew, a lawyer who kept toying with his cell phone as if he meant to use it in church. Time pitched Alastair backwards like salt tossed for good luck, but it was bitter salt from the ebb tide of his marriage when he'd fallen into young Claire's life. He watched her greet John Miller who could have been Lyle as a young man with his unruly wheat-sheaf of hair and narrow face, his eyes the soft and faded blue of an old, comfortable shirt. John's gaze was more wary, less guileless than his dad's. Long ago, when Alastair was still married to Nora, he'd let his hand rest on her stomach, knowing she was pregnant with John. Only it wasn't his child.

Alastair had found a measure of peace since then.

And yet.

Forgiveness takes your whole life. After the service he went up to Nora.

"My condolences," he said.

"Thank you," she replied.

"I hope you'll get some rest," he told her.

Nora smoothed a stray hair back from her forehead. "I saw you looking for Grace," she said. Her tone had a laser precision that didn't invite rebuttal. *Nora, is it anything to you?* How it hurt him, that years after their marriage ended, she'd observe him with such telling insight, letting him know how astute she was with her eyes, if not her heart.

5

She's upset, Alastair thought. *Not herself.*

She introduced her son who shook his hand, and he recalled Lyle's first son Todd, his lost boy. *Todd would have grown up to look like John,* he thought. The young man seemed bereft, yet he could feel the quickness of his eyes as if they were Todd's eyes playing with the world. He saw in them a hint of the dead boy's prescience, the same edge of contempt that troubled him once in a child so young. It haunted him still, that Todd might have glimpsed how his life would end, how an inattentive man would kill him. *All your life you'll carry the weight of what you did,* the judge said.

He'd wanted so much for Lyle to have another son.

"I didn't catch your name," said John.

"Al Luce."

John turned his back to him, took Nora's elbow, and walked with her to the waiting limousine.

2

IN SIMPLER TIMES, Alastair and Nora had been man and wife. He cast a backward glance from the new century to 1959, to a world at peace, to their marriage of thirteen years. On Long Island Sound, on the nearby Linden shore, the sand rippled like a flag, starred with a careful, neat expanse of canvas umbrellas, collapsible wooden beach chairs, straw baskets, mothers and kids. It was a hot and rainless June, and at the library, Nora watched the lazy breeze nudge the window curtain by her desk. She had a fan, but she would have liked air conditioning, as they had at the movies. Her favourite films were *Thirty Seconds Over Tokyo* and *The Bridge on the River Kwai*. She'd been an air-raid warden during the war and on hot nights she'd get Alastair to take her to action films. After a while, she went alone.

Times were good and one neighbour bought a Chrysler with vast, gull-like fins. Soon there were more in the neighbourhood, as if the first one had laid eggs and hatched a flock. On the radio, there was a song called "Quiet Village," full of muted drums, squawking cockatoos and monkeys. *Exotic,* said the announcer. *You can just picture the jungle.* This, it seemed to Alastair, was all that anyone wanted to know of the world.

When they were younger, he and Nora had ambled through summers like this one. On the patio she'd stand, shaping hamburgers for the grill, separating each with a waxed-paper square, her eyes far away. Alastair could feel in her words a stirring of the air, as if Nora herself were drifting like a breeze — her feet rising up from the ground, the patty, its paper dividers, napkins, plastic cutlery and paper plates fluttering away like blossom petals in a wind. He had married a woman who from time to time took flight, whose imagination could light on the world like a butterfly on the sweet inside of a flower. Because he was an artist, he'd counted this a gift in her, one that he loved.

He remembered a day when Nora's eyes had been distracted by Lyle Miller in the yard beyond their fence. Alastair had noticed his empty pants leg, the way he'd eased himself out the door like a kid on his first pair of skates. How odd it was that the man's misfortune made him think of the northern lakes of childhood, cool even in the long, bright days of Canadian summer. He'd looked away, his mind drifting through boreal forest.

"More than his share of troubles, Lyle," said Nora.

Grace was playing with Todd, and he could hear their startled, gleeful yells. Toddlers in swimsuits, they were running around the nozzle of the hose, the fine spray Lyle set on them. Alastair loved their innocent dance, their shrieks of joy.

"Look at the kids," he said.

He was still looking, even now.

"They play so well together," Nora replied.

Grace often went to the beach with Todd and his mom. Busy as the town's librarian, Nora hadn't time to take her daughter swimming. As for Alastair, he didn't care to lounge in the coastal heat and he never took to the indolent style of the Linden shore. After work he'd sometimes drive the truck a few miles north on the Post Road, turning off at Rye, driving past the crammed-full park to its silent and much smaller twin, a nearby scrap of land that jutted out into the sound like a hitchhiker's thumb. Here he'd found an abandoned space, the sound-water clotted with seaweed, the sand rocky and uncombed. Yet he'd found peace in the gulls' cries, the brackish air, the tangle of unruly grasses. Alone he'd sit by the edge of the beach where he'd stare at the water and relax with a beer, imagining the children, Grace and Todd, skipping in the froth of the waves.

3

NORA HAD BONFIRE HAIR and eyes that flashed green like a cat's in the dark. He'd met her during the war, in a munitions plant on Long Island while she was waiting for Lyle Miller to come home from Europe. She'd volunteered for Civil Defence and spent lunch hours hanging posters in the shop. *Help me win the war!* she yelled. Alastair had no interest in the war. He liked her sassiness, its current running through her veins, and he wondered at her optimistic passion for the sorry world that had drawn them together for a time. She was sky to his humble earth, a wild wind blowing through his spirit

It was his good fortune that poor Lyle Miller lost a leg on D-Day, then fell in love with his English nurse. Nora grieved, but not for long. In love, Alastair pondered the war that skittered along like a twister, ripping lives apart, tossing the shards together in a heap. Nora'd hit him like flying timber, and he fell, pinned under the beam. Or maybe it was the opposite, and he had crushed her. At first, he blamed it on the war.

* * *

They moved to the town of Linden, just north of New York City, where Al began his house-painting business. It prospered, and he bought his supplies at the bulk-discount rate from Miller's hardware. The Luces and the Millers were neighbours, and their common interests helped ease what might have been an awkward situation. Along with Lyle and his wife Mary, Nora lived her life on alert for shots unheard and for air raid sirens that would never sound again. The three of them mulled over the threat of communist subversion and Nora wrote warning letters to her senators and congressmen. Al sensed in his wife a *frisson* of excitement, that she'd be an air-raid warden once again and prowl the wildcat rooftops, her binoculars scanning the skies for enemy planes. To her chagrin, this cold-war assignment was left to the men.

Nora felt sure there was a fear of woman's lightness, of the gust of wind that might sweep her off the roof, her binoculars slipping out of her hand, the strap looping over the wing of a passing plane; a fear that she'd lose her grip, let go, launch herself toward the razzle-dazzle starlight when the times called for gravity, the *thunk* of weighty things: Iron Curtains, ICBMs, Strategies of Containment. All this she told Alastair.

Lighter than air she was still.

"Wouldn't you rather dance?" he asked.

Nora became a librarian. She stocked the shelves with American history, and Lyle Miller came to read. War vet, Legion Post Commander; once a week he hop-stepped up the library stairs and she waited for him, her green eyes alight, her hair on fire.

* * *

Alastair's property backed up on the woods. He remembered walking along the treed path with Nora as autumn leaves sifted down and branches snapped underfoot. After years living in southern New York State, he still remarked on the brittleness of trees. How frail they were, these American woods, the twigs of oak and tulip and sycamore, and he felt in them a restlessness that could hold neither the wind nor the leaves. He longed for the sturdy arms of Canadian spruce and jack pine, the trees' unchanging calm in the bitterest winter. Nora was pregnant, and he gripped her arm.

"I won't blow away," she said.

I might, he thought.

He'd dreamt about his father in Port Radium, Canada's far north. In his dream, the sheet-lightning was so bright that he could see through the man to his skeleton; its ribs like the rungs of a ladder to nowhere. *A light,* he heard his father say, *that's carried in the bones.*

On TV, they said the Russians had the Bomb.

"I worry," said Alastair.

Nora laughed. "Don't. We have it, too."

"That's why I worry," he said.

Nora stroked his arm, and he glanced at the curve of her stomach, staring with apprehension at the dark, tumescent clouds.

Bone of my bone.

***

He slept with his head on Nora's stomach, and he dreamt that the child inside her was covered in poisoned snow.

In the morning, Nora asked him to pick up coals for the barbecue and a case of beer. They were cooking out with Lyle and Mary and the Bernards, did he forget? Their neighbours came over that warm June evening. Mary brought coleslaw and a jello-mould salad.

"If I were young again," Lyle sighed. He poured himself a cold one.

"You'd do what?" said Alastair.

"I'd fight. Get the commies out of Europe."

Alastair flipped the steak on the grill. He said nothing. Lyle chugged down his beer.

"Waddya say, pal?"

"Good exercise," said Al.

"Huh?"

"War's outdoors. Get your fresh air."

"You Canucks," said Lyle. "Life's a friggin' moose hunt."

"You Yanks," said Alastair.

"What's wrong with us?"

Alastair left the steak alone, guzzled his beer and tossed the empty can in the trash. He smiled.

"You don't know?"

"No."

"Imperialist warmongers."

"That's not funny," said Nora afterwards.

"It's Canadian humour."

"It's disrespectful," she told him.

"Of what?"

Nora told him he knew damn well.

In truth, he knew nothing, except for the fact that he came from a powerless country where his father had been a socialist. *Here comes a dreamer*, said his mother when his dad returned home from meetings, but on her lips this was a benediction. Alastair heard the words she didn't speak: *What'll become of his dreams?* His father loved to read, and he'd left his son a stack of books: Reed and Trotsky and labour leaders whose names he couldn't remember. Alastair had read these, but he'd found words to be like medicine, most powerful when taken in, less so when sent out like vapour into the air. In his adopted country, he had little to say. When he found time, he read.

As a youth, he'd taught himself to paint, finding colour stronger, more exact than words. Yet these days, all he could conjure up was snow and ice, and all he could see and feel and taste was an occluding swirl of chilled white dust. That was how he saw the world, as if a schoolmate were clapping two huge erasers full of blackboard chalk, the wind whiting out every image, ice pellets choking his words. It felt as if life would end in a chill white cloud, in the gust and scribble of a whiteness on the vast sky.

His snow-child, its blood white.

* * *

"You'll have the FBI at our door," said Nora.

She watched Alastair throw the Ban-the-Bomb signs in the trunk, then drive off to New York City. Later she told Lyle Miller that her husband was a nervous man, that he'd grown up poor in a Canadian mining town, that his father had to ride the rails for work. She didn't talk about his politics.

More than once, Al marched.

"New-dad heebie-jeebies," said Lyle when he found out. "Too smart to be a Red." He patted her shoulder. His touch moved like wind in her hair.

* * *

Grace was born whole and well. She was two days old when Alastair lifted her from her mother's arms and held her. Tiny she was, eyes shut, the folds of her skin rumpled and pink like the half-open petals of a rose, her miniature hands curled into perfection. He touched them, feeling in their softness the ferns of the northern bogs in spring. Her eyes opened into an unfocussed, infinite blue, as if she were a part of the sky, a mysterious apparition. *How is it you're here?* said the touch of his hand. Ten fingers, ten toes, two seeing eyes, more than enough to heal a wound, a gift to sustain him. *Grace, yes.* He kissed her forehead and handed her back to Nora. For a while he forgot the power of light, the fearful dust that fell from the sky to the grass.

4

IN GOOD WEATHER, Alastair was a busy man. He worked alone and as he painted houses, he could feel colour humming under the bright surfaces of everything he touched as if colour were a sound, an eerie music. His was a humble job, sprucing things up and no more, and he was intrigued by the sense of immanent life that wanted to speak through the ordinary tools of work. At home he tried to paint with new colours, but he never could. Instead they found their way into his sleep where they turned his dreams into brilliant and disturbing canvases, patchworks of colour like a TV image poorly tuned. Once he saw a man's face, his own stepfather. The following morning, the man died. In his sleep, he saw bright lightning, blue-razor sharp, as it struck and lit a sailboat mast, and he heard the hiss of it igniting like a match. Opening the paper at breakfast, he read how a freak storm arose on the sound, killing two of his neighbours.

Alastair began to drink before he went to bed.

"It's not as if it's your fault, what you dream," said Nora. "Just don't tell anyone."

"I won't."

"They'll lock you up if you do."

There were times he wished he could find someone to help him.

Alcohol made his life twist and fold like a glove that was meant to fit a soothing hand, meant to adapt to the flexing of its fist. He drank in quiet, at the end of a day, and his troubling dreams occurred less often. Sober when he worked, he hid his lone weakness as best he could at home. He accepted it as part of who he was, and he often mused that had he been American-born, he might have been a stronger man, a better match for Nora's spirit. Instead, he lived with a northern austerity, a patient bending to the weight of life as if he were a spruce bough limber enough to shuck its load of snow. He couldn't console his wife for the passage of time, for the loss of her youth to a man like himself.

For Grace he wanted the strength and passion of her mother. She was four years old when he put a red crayon in her hand, guiding it along the page to form the letters of her name: G-R-A-C-E. He pointed to each of the letters and named them. When he put his hand on hers again, she pulled away.

"By myself," she said. Grace pushed hard, her crayon making bloody gashes.

"Good girl."

Grace started scribbling again. She was a tiny generator, light and power unstoppable, her dark crayon marking the page. When she was done, she clutched her drawing to her chest, her eyes grave.

"Let me see," said Alastair.

Grace looked troubled, and he could feel her reluctance as she handed him the paper. It was covered with huge crimson splotches, like the indelible stains of crushed berries on linen. In her eyes he glimpsed the fear and bewilderment of a small traveller who had stumbled into a whirlwind, into a fury much larger than her tiny self. She looked sombre and frail, in need of protection. He reached out to pat her head, but she raised her arm to cover her face, backing away from him in fear.

He noticed a bruise on her arm. Later, he spoke to Nora.

"She has no discipline," his wife said. "She's more than I can handle."

"She's four years old," said Alastair.

"She takes after you."

"So don't hit her, then," said Alastair. "Hit me."

* * *

Painful as it was, Alastair realized that to Nora's mind, Grace was a plain little girl, as grubby as an old potato. She'd claw at the mud, eat dirt, and soil her clothes. Her favourite song was "Old MacDonald Had a Farm." Nora cringed at the nonsense words, the barnyard sounds. Dirt made her cry in frustration. Wanting to protect Grace and ease Nora's distress, Alastair hired a neighbour's oldest daughter to babysit her after school. Betty-Ann Bernard was a talented painter whose grooming was impeccable.

"I'd put that kid in the Marines," said Nora, "if they took girls."

She's a kidder, he thought.

* * *

Alastair gave Grace paper and paint. As a baby, she'd sat mesmerized, watching him painting scenes that Nora liked: Canada's chill lakes, boreal forests, rough mining towns laden with the weight and heft of blue-greens and fiery golds. He couldn't paint like that anymore. With Grace at his side, it felt as if colour were seeping out of his veins from a self-inflicted wound he couldn't bind. He was painting as a miner would dig, gutting his life to the quick. He re-painted the north of his youth a savage blue that he spread with a knife. Of his father and his mining town, his hands exuded a silver iridescence streaked with black. Nora peeked over his shoulder.

"There's nothing there," she said.

There was. There had to be.

"I watched my father die," he said. "That's there."

Grace was smearing black paint on paper.

"Don't make a mess," said Nora.

* * *

He painted Grace, her grave and luminous image flowing out of his hand. This portrait stunned him, as if its beauty were a stranger's work. He stopped, noticing the wildness he'd caught in her eyes, a veiled insanity that frightened him. He hadn't the craft to capture it all. He drank as he worked.

* * *

Grace was as bright as the head of a nail and all of nine when she first grabbed a bucket of paint and let her furious work run wild on crates and garbage pails, wash-buckets, and dead tires scrounged from neighbours' garages. Other kids thought she was weird, and they avoided her. Grace said she didn't care. The neighbours shrugged and said she'd outgrow it. Alastair hoped she wouldn't.

A year or so later he was mowing the lawn when he saw her across the yard at Lyle and Mary Miller's, painting their back fence lavender and red. *Thank God those two are out of town,* he thought. He watched the scene, as if Grace's behaviour and its consequences were two lazy vessels, becalmed and rudderless, far away from each other. *Who the hell said "Property is theft?" He'd like this.*

"I'll kill you!"

Nora's voice scraped the air, then stopped dead, like an airplane's conked-out engine. He hadn't even seen her until she ran up to Grace, grabbed her, and smacked her face. Grace reeled and fell. Nora told her to go to her room. She glared at Alastair.

"You bastard, I'll brain you, too."

"What for?"

"You couldn't fucking well stop her?"

"It's mischief," said Alastair.

"Like hell, Alastair Luce. She's wrecking someone's property. And you stand there and do nothing?"

Nora was weeping. Alastair put his arm around her and walked her into the house. She slammed the door and glared at him.

"You let me do the dirty work," she said. "You don't goddamn well care."

"I do care."

"What kind of a father doesn't make rules?"

"She's just a kid. It's harmless."

"Is booze harmless? Is your bad example harmless?"

She strode out of the room.

* * *

When he spoke to Grace, she told him she was sorry.

"Why did you mess up the fence?" he asked her.

"I don't know." Grace started to cry.

"We'll have to fix it." He put his hand on her chin, turning her face so that he could meet her eyes. "Mom didn't mean it," he said. "She was upset."

Grace looked away.

5

ALASTAIR FELT TROUBLED about Lyle's fence, but more so about his own indifference, as if Grace were expressing a thing he'd kept well-hidden, an inarticulate fury — at what, he was uncertain. He didn't belong to these people, to their preoccupation with prim backyards, politics, and battle. Yet he wasn't alone with his feelings of disquiet. Lyle Miller was also silent these days, at low tide, as if he were pulling away from the rocky shore of his own life. A fastidious man, he didn't seem to care about Grace's mischief. *You got a tomboy there, is all,* he said to Al, as if his peeling fence were too good a temptation to pass up. He insisted on re-painting it himself. He was always at work on something these days, as if life were a building project, as if down at the store he had a good-sized bolt that might pull together a bad join, as in a marriage, say. Al respected Lyle, whose mind and hands kept busy, as if screws and clamps were sufficient to mend whatever broken part of himself he couldn't fix.

One of these days, Lyle would snap out of his mood. Then he'd yank Todd out of Grace's life like a hammer's claw pulling a nail from wood. Two years younger, Todd was her only friend on the street. Al decided that for his daughter's sake he had to find some way to compensate his neighbour. He mulled this over as he painted, aware that the two kids were watching him that day, as silent as a pair of cats in church.

Todd looked forlorn.

"Paint me, too," Todd said.

"Daddy, yes."

It was almost too easy. It was nicer than painting a fence. He felt for Todd. The poor kid seemed too alone these days, lost in a silence larger than he was. As for Todd's father, it was much the same. Loneliness was such a shapeless garment, a loose fit that hid the flesh and bones of loss and hurt, and he wondered how it was that all of them were so afflicted. With a pang of guilt, he thought of Nora, her unspent passion at a simmer, boiling over into a froth of worry over Soviet sputniks and science education. He saw how well she got on with Lyle, but chose to put it out of his mind, afraid that her anxiety was rubbing off on him. His own desire for Nora came and went. His loneliness was his own fault.

How desolate he was.

Todd Miller looked up at him. "Mr. Luce?"

"Yes?"

"You'll paint me, huh?"

Alastair stroked the young boy's hair, the silk of it, life spinning a new thing. He had to hope.

Afterwards he spoke to Lyle, explaining to him that one paint job deserved another, so to compensate for Grace's mischief, he'd like to do a portrait of Todd. Lyle was intrigued. Over the next two weeks, Alastair sketched the boy and then began to paint him. Engrossed in his work, he drank less, forgetting himself as he peered into the depths of the child before him. How was it that a nine-year-old could remain so still, so focused on sitting for his portrait? Alastair asked himself what Todd was so desperate to communicate, so clear was his mood and his expression. One day, close to completing the portrait, he felt a jolt of fright that leapt from the boy and into his hand. Not a confused and wounded gaze emerging, but a look of terror and reproach in Todd's pale eyes. Dismissal and contempt in this child. Not grief.

How dare you? Alastair painted this.

A few hours later, Lyle came to get his son. He leaned against the doorway, one hand on his cane. He glanced from the painting to Todd.

"That you?" he asked.

Todd didn't answer.

"Let's put a smile on that face," said Lyle. "You want Mr. Luce to paint a *happy* boy."

Alastair asked Lyle how things were going.

"Okay," he said.

"You need a hand, you call, huh?"

"Got two good ones of my own." He started for the door. "Gonna be a great portrait," he said. "Todd's shy, that's all. C'mere, son." Todd stood next to his dad. "Give Mr. Luce a big smile. 'Let a smile be your umbrella.' Remember that song, Al?"

Al didn't.

Todd smiled.

"You did well, son," said Mr. Miller.

"Thank you, sir."

"Atta boy." He clapped Todd on the back. The boy relaxed and the hard look vanished from his pale bright eyes. Fair-haired and freckled, he grinned like a Norman Rockwell kid, set for a game of ball.

Alastair glanced once more at the painting. Todd's eyes stared back. It was then he realized that something had transpired between himself and the boy, some wordless insight that only an artist's brush could hold. For a moment, time had vanished, as if Todd were dangling over the infinity of his own life like an insect captured in a spider's web.

No words in response. Just that look.

Thanks a bunch, Mr. Luce.
Fuckyoufuckyoufuckyou.

* * *

A day or two passed and it was Nora's birthday, but she told Al that she didn't want to celebrate. She had to work late and the following morning was a work day, besides which she'd have to get Grace out the door for summer school because she'd gone and flunked math. Even so, Al welcomed her home with chocolates and roses and a Montovani album and he reminded her that tomorrow morning, young Claire Bernard was coming around to walk Grace to school so Nora wouldn't have to drop her off. Claire was a generous kid, Betty-Ann's younger sister. She'd been helping Grace out with math. More than that. Grace said Claire picked up on things. She'd showed her his painting of Todd, and Claire had said, *I can almost hear him talking to us.*

Alastair felt grateful for her kindness.

He put the disk on the turntable and held Nora close to him. It had been a while since they'd drawn this close. He'd forgotten her warmth, the sweet aliveness of her flesh.

"I'm not much of a dancer anymore," she said.

"Not true," said Alastair.

Nora was moving through him like the wind. He held her tight.

"I guess I'm tired," she said.

Alastair kissed her hair. "You're still hot stuff."

"Think so?"

"Birthday girl. What do you want most?"

"I want to start my life again."

But not with me, he thought. The words fell into his mind like pebbles, the beginnings of an avalanche.

He took her in his arms and held her with care, as you might

23

hold silence. She did not respond to his embrace. In her was a sorrow he couldn't penetrate, a grievous story that he felt he must have written, but couldn't read. Like having lousy eyesight, like trying to read the letters on the chart while the doctor flips lens after lens — *not this one; no, not that one.* Nothing would help a man that close to blindness. Why couldn't he see? Perplexed, he'd blamed their confusions on the war that had hurled them together like flying debris from a bomb-blast of a ruined home. It had cracked the foundations of hope, made fissures in its sheltering walls, pinned them under its collapsing roof-beams. Of all of life's generous gifts, sex was the only one that had shifted the unbearable weight of so much sorrow. He wondered how it was they'd lost that, too.

Besides, Grace was too much for Nora. He could do better as a father. He feared for his child. Yet he could return none of what his wife had lost. He took her hands and pressed them to his lips, but he felt nothing, as if she had vanished.

"No more booze," he said.

"It's more than that."

He hadn't the courage to ask her what it was.

He sensed she wanted him to ask, but his lips couldn't form the words. *Do you want to leave me, Nora?* He touched her cheek and his finger traced the furrows of her brow, the fine lines and wrinkles around her eyes as if he were a blind man reading braille. He couldn't let himself imagine that she'd sleep with Lyle.

"I love you still," he said.

She grabbed his hand and put it on her stomach.

"What is it?" he asked, but he knew.

"Use your imagination," said Nora, and she wept.

It isn't mine. He handed her a box of tissues. He told her he'd sleep in the guest room.

Families Live Alone

6

M Y NAME IS CLAIRE BERNARD, and I work as a reporter in Toronto. Mom used to say that I was born with a notebook in my hand. If I'd been hatched today, I would have been texting before I could crawl. You'll understand what I'm getting at if you remember the osmosis experiment you did in high school biology, water trickling through "a semi-permeable membrane." That was me, as porous as a sponge. Without even trying, I mopped up everything the adults said. If you'd wrung me out, you'd have had a flood of gossip, rumour, innuendo, and grief. I wrote to keep sane.

It was 1960. I was fourteen years old and the coastal air of Linden was too hot for good sense or decent conversation, but hot enough for outrageous things to happen. At that time, I was staying out of the house because I couldn't handle my sister Betty-Ann's inane provocations. The two of us took turns babysitting our little neighbour, Todd Miller, but it riled my sister that I'd end up playing with both him and his friend Grace. Five blocks away, but it felt to Betty-Ann as if I were defiling our home by stepping into the Luce abode. It happened that I'd borrowed one of Mr. Luce's socialist books when I was visiting Grace, and Betty-Ann picked it up and held it at arm's length, as if it were covered with rat droppings from the last bubonic plague.

He's not even American, she said of the bearded farmer

on the cover. *Neither is your French perfume*, I said. And on it went.

I'd just finished freshman year of high school near the top of my class, so to cheer me on, my parents picked up the tab for a summer workshop in journalism. At the other end of the spectrum, poor Grace had flunked math and had to repeat her course in summer school. She was depressed about it, but I offered to walk with her to class and help her with her homework. Grace's class started at nine a.m., an hour earlier than mine, but her school was closer, so I could drop her off on my way to Linden High. Besides, I liked leaving in the early morning to escape the worst of the heat.

On this particular day, when I went to pick up Grace, I could sense something amiss. In the kitchen, the air itself seemed to bend under the weight of silence. You wouldn't have dared to strike a match in that room; it might have exploded. You could almost hear the dangerous hiss of gas escaping.

There was a bouquet of roses on the table. *Someone's had a fight*, I thought. *Wanted to make up, and it didn't work.* Mrs. Luce was pouring her husband coffee. *Would you like some,* she asked me. She didn't say good morning. I said yes.

Across from Mr. Luce sat Grace, looking sullen. She was drawing on her napkin.

"Eat up," said her mother. "Don't dawdle, you'll be late."

Mr. Luce was watching as his daughter sketched. So was I. Mrs. Luce came up behind her and yanked the pencil out of her hand. Grace resumed nibbling on her toast.

"Gracie," said her dad.

"Uh-huh?"

"We'll draw some tonight."

"She has a test tomorrow," her mother said.

He picked up her napkin and looked at the sketch of his tired eyes gazing at nothing in particular. He showed it to me in silence. Putting it in his pocket, he must have wondered why the hell she needed math.

"Nice," he told her.

"You'll never get to school on time," said Mrs. Luce. Grace got up, gave the chair a hard shove, and stomped off to get her books.

"She is — impossible," said her mother.

"Nora, it's —"

She looked at her husband with amusement, disgust, pleasure — I wasn't sure which. I wanted to leave, I felt I had no business watching this, and yet I was mesmerized by the crackle of argument, the quick, hot spike of sexual longing, the flash of desire in a man's face and his wife's triumphant look, that she'd aroused him. I shivered in the heat.

"I'll drive Grace," said her mother. "It's getting too damn late."

Grace came back with her books. "Let's go." Mrs. Luce grabbed her by the shoulder, squeezing her skin.

"That *hurts*."

"That's fat. You're putting on weight. That's why I wanted Claire to walk with you. Your skirt's so tight, it's indecent."

"It's not indecent. It's the style."

Mr. Luce eyed his wife, her flesh snug against the sleek cut of her dress.

Now look at me, Mr. Luce. Not a thought, but my body's voice, and it stunned me. It happened that I was wearing a crisp white skirt with a matching white-and-navy belt and sleeveless blouse. *How nice you look*, my mom had said at breakfast. Only this wasn't nice. This was crazy in its vastness like the laws of gravity and angular momentum, this slow turning in his direction, a planet orbiting a greater sun. It wasn't so much wanting to turn his way. It was having to.

Only just then, Mr. Luce had his hands full.

"Gracie," he said.

"What?"

"Don't talk back to your mother. Say you're sorry."

Grace apologized.

Mrs. Luce was fussing with her hair, glancing in the hall mirror. Mr. Luce looked pained. He was watching her smile at herself, her tongue moistening her lips.

7

YOU MIGHT SAY MR. LUCE had a reputation. Yet in those fearful, cold-war days, the gossip had nothing to do with sex. "Kind of a rebel is Al, that's all," Mom said, whenever the Millers would call him a Red.

I knew about the Reds in Soviet Russia. But a rebel, now that was different. From my vantage-point at age fourteen, it was easy to conclude that Mr. Luce must have been lonely, introspective, misunderstood — slightly off to the side of bad, meaning he had a good heart and wasn't bad at all.

Besides, Mr. Luce was as good-looking as they come. A dangerous kind of workingman handsome — black hair, pitch-dark eyes, firm jaw, muscle, brawn, and sweat, all *man*. Stuff more or less deodorized out of Linden's beach-club boys, future corporate lawyers, tanned and bland.

Even better, Mr. Luce was foreign-born. He'd grown up in the Canadian wilderness, a place I imagined as magnificent — glittering rock, lakes like mirrors reflecting spruce and pine, woods alive with wildcats and black bears. It made him a solitary man. In his spare time he painted and read books. He never went to the Memorial Day parade, never saluted the flag or sang *God Bless America*. He never argued politics, never excused or explained himself. He just didn't follow our customs. My dad said he was a pink Canuck, but my mother's sharp voice would snip the thread of gossip.

"He's got a lot on his mind," she'd say. And that was that.
I wanted to be his friend. Why? I was lonely, I guess. It was a stirring of the heart, and that was all.

My sister saw things differently. "I hate Mr. Luce," she said.

"How come?" I asked.

"He's a dumb dago."

"Italian," I insisted. Except that he wasn't.

"Italian like you," she snapped.

"Like Marcello Mastroianni," I retorted.

What the hell did Italian have to do with anything?

"Alastair's a Scots name," my mother said.

"Luce could be Loo-chay," said Betty-Ann.

In fact we were part-Italian; Bernardinis on my dad's side. The offending suffix had been snipped off my grandfather's name at Ellis Island and we became Bernards, like those brandy-toting canines in the Alps. Stylish Betty-Ann, who worked summers for Chanel, was often asked if the name were French. *Mais, oui*, she'd say.

"Betty Ber-nar-di-ni," I said, rolling the r's.

"Loo-chay looks like the Mafia," said Betty-Ann.

My sister's boyfriend was very blond and in uniform, with a mirror-shine to his leather boots. He looked like the Gestapo. I bit my tongue.

Betty-Ann hated Mr. Luce the minute she'd set eyes on him. He must have looked her over more than once when she babysat Grace. My sister was beautiful but she despised leers from tradesmen, while she put up with — and even welcomed — stares from college men. The distinction was hers.

Because she was a Fine Arts major, she got to sit on the judges' panel for the Linden Summer Art Show. Each year Mr. Luce would enter a landscape or two. He'd never win anything. Once she took me with her on her judging rounds.

"What's wrong?" I asked her. She was staring at one of his oils.

"Oh, God. See for yourself."

"Is it something in the painting?"

"It's so *clichéd*. It's..." Her voice trailed off. She was cringing, as if his hapless technique threatened her with its thick paint, its crude application of colour. I couldn't figure out why it should.

"It's not contagious, is it?" I asked.

"What's not contagious?"

"Folk art." I wasn't prepared to call it bad.

Betty-Ann sighed. "If you only realized," she said, "how much I don't want to *fall into* that."

Her intensity took me aback. What had rattled her wasn't Mr. Luce, but something far more primitive, as if she were the first *Homo Sapiens*, rejoicing in her marvellous brain and upright stance, praying to God she wouldn't spoil it all by growing a tail. "What don't you want to fall into?"

"You'll never understand. It's —"

Her voice faded off, but her eyes were as sharp as a gambler's at a crapshoot, her ear cocked for the clickety-click of the gaming wheel, the sound of an invisible shuttle with its random weaving of her DNA into lovely spiralling patterns. Poor Betty-Ann. She must have known that her lustrous blonde mane was a recessive gene, a fluke that saved her from the coarseness of black Italian hair. She might "fall into" worse things. Under her slender model's shape, a peasant woman's fat might emerge; under her genteel American speech was the hard-wired memory of faulty English and dialect words; behind her love for a gentle, fair-haired man was the danger that she'd throw him aside for an earthy son-of-a-bitch like Mr. Luce.

He must have given her one hell of a buzz.

She didn't know her own good luck, I thought then.

* * *

Grace once showed me a corner of the basement full of her

father's books. They were old, older than the Second World War, and to me their age was a poignant and sorrowful thing. An avid reader, I didn't know what to make of these volumes, mildewed and suffering from neglect. They had an air of melancholy, like old folks on park benches. I picked one up. *What we want for ourselves, we wish for all,* it said. It was from Canada, the cover depicting a group of farmers. I leafed through a few more volumes.

"Hey, Gracie, these are *socialist.*"

"I know. Mom wants to burn 'em."

"Like the Inquisition, huh?"

"What's that?"

I didn't go into it. It made me wonder how Mr. and Mrs. Luce had ended up together. Mom told me that Grace's great-grandparents had been in a general strike in Winnipeg, Canada, and that her granddad was a communist. Her dad's side of the family tree came with a serpent and an apple. I yearned for a bite.

"Those books are boring," said Grace.

"No, they're not." I had it in mind to borrow a few.

"Show you what's neat about my dad." She took me into his shed to see his paintings. One had an odd luminosity that I found disturbing.

"Dad's an artist," she said. "It's *supposed* to disturb you."

A few minutes later, Mr. Luce walked in. I pointed to the painting that had troubled me.

"Why does it look that way?" I asked.

He hesitated. "It's just — how things look."

What things? I felt uneasy.

"It's called *The Star Inside the Rock.*"

It moved me. Yet it was a sad light, and I told him that, too. He smiled a little.

"The world is sad sometimes," he replied.

8

M RS. LUCE PULLED OUT of the driveway with Grace, who was running late for her class. I was on my way out the door when Mr. Luce offered me a ride. He had a painting job at Beaches Point, near the Linden town line, where the high school was. "It's nice and cool in the truck," he said.

I heard a car door slam one house over. It was Mrs. Miller behind the wheel, with Todd in the front seat. She volunteered at the hospital, my mom said, and on those days, she'd drop Todd off at the bus stop for day-camp. Mrs. Miller looked grim. *Everyone's out of it today*, I thought. Todd waved.

I waved back, then turned to Alastair, told him I'd love a ride.

It would be a relief, to get away from here. The air had become leaden, electric. I felt exposed, like a tree in an open field, about to draw lightning.

I got in the truck, rolled down the window and was struck dumb. Fifteen minutes alone with Mr. Luce, and I didn't have a thing to say. I wanted to sound intelligent, to discuss some issue pertinent to the world we shared. The future of capitalism. Mr. Khrushchev's policies on Berlin. *Are you really a socialist? Did your parents ever tell you about the general strike?* Or maybe something more personal. *Tell me about the north country. Have you ever seen a bear?* Tongue-tied. Handsome bad-guy rebel, good at heart, said my insides, melting like a Hershey bar in a furnace.

Only I'd never sat in a truck before.

"It's high off the ground," I said.

"You get used to it."

Gee, did I feel like a dimwit.

I stared out the window. A hot day all right, the cicadas sawing away as Mr. Luce pulled the truck out of his driveway on Pinewood Road, then turned right two blocks down, on to the slope of Rose Hill Drive, the main street east into Linden.

I tried again. I decided that Khrushchev could wait.

"Grace is talented, huh?" I said.

"Very." He paused. "Glad you could help her this summer."

"It's no trouble."

"You're a good friend for Gracie."

"Well I just feel that marks aren't everything. She's smart in other ways."

"I tell her mother that," he said.

Mr. Luce grew silent. He drove, his eyes fixed on the road ahead. With the mention of Mrs. Luce, it felt as if another presence had entered the truck, one that he didn't welcome. I noticed the grip of his hands on the wheel, a glint of anger in his eyes. At first I wondered if I'd said something wrong, and then I remembered the mood in the kitchen that morning. It had a sound, *ftttzzss-zzzip*, like putting a wet finger in a light socket. It had a colour, too, burnt-black.

This had nothing to do with me.

We rolled along through what used to be a thick old woods, each of the street-names attached to a knoll or a ridge or a *kill* in Dutch, the hidden places where those settlers found water. The homes here were built of stone and wood-frame, and their lots were so treed that the houses were starting to look a bit like trees themselves. I told Mr. Luce that.

"You've got that artist's eye," he said. "Like Gracie."

I went soft and moist as custard. They say that sex starts in the brain, no kidding. Yet I felt shy and uncomfortable, wondering if the brain could dissolve in the body's involuntary longing, like a giant Alka-Seltzer in a glass of water. In truth, I didn't feel ready for this part of life. I wanted a grown-up friend, and that was all. This new set of feelings made me anxious.

"Thank you," I said. "But Gracie's the real artist. She needs friends like herself. It must get lonely for her."

"I think you're right."

"Especially being an only child."

Mr. Luce took in his breath. He said nothing. He looked upset.

What did I say? I wondered.

At last he spoke.

"Not for long," he said.

I took a deep breath. "Oh wow," I said, but not "congratulations," because in his voice I heard despair.

* * *

Not knowing what to say, I eyed my surroundings, trying to enjoy riding shotgun (as my dad called it), high up in the truck. So the Luces were expecting. No doubt that explained the weird mood in their kitchen. More kids were being born these days; I knew that because my dad kept saying that this charming old forest road needed traffic signs, that they'd have to put them up for the swarm of baby-boom kids and their anxious parents. This wooded part of town was quaint, like a sweet child's face that would soon be pimpled with traffic lights and crosswalks; like those barnyard wagon wheels propped up on tree trunks or lamp posts, like the one just off Rose Hill with a corny sign, *The Wheeler Residence.*

Mayor Wheeler. Betty-Ann was dating his son.

The silence made me anxious. "Lots of kids in the neighbourhood now," I said. I pulled out my handkerchief. My hands felt moist with dread.

"Grace's mother —" He didn't finish the sentence.

He's worried how she'll treat the baby. She's so hard on Grace.

"Grace takes after you," I said.

"We're two bad apples." He smiled.

"I can babysit the new one," I said.

Mr. Luce gripped the wheel, his truck picking up speed. *Four goddamn rotten apples,* said his eyes. *Counting you and Nora.* All because I reminded him of what he feared, making the child real by offering to babysit. I had to go and blabber like that, and now he looked upset. I felt glad for the space between us, sitting as close to the door as I could get.

It was a steep roll down Rose Hill, and up ahead a half-mile was the turnoff at Benson's Thicket. The road had no name, and the turn was almost invisible, but drivers who knew the route gave the side road a quick glance and picked up speed for a downward roll into town. Mr. Luce was no exception. The wheels flew.

Poor Mr. Luce, I thought. *He's afraid to have another baby. He's afraid that Mrs. Luce will —*

I never finished the thought. A car came shooting out of the Benson's Thicket side road, and Mr. Luce hit the brake, swerved and lost control, heading straight for the curb where a boy stood waiting for the day-camp bus, and I'm thinking in that crazy way you do when trouble's snuffing and growling and ready to rip you to bits, *couldn't his mother have driven him? What's he doing, standing there?*

The brain's last little burble before you die.

The other vehicle sped through the intersection while Alastair's truck veered to the right and jumped the curb. The last thing I remember was the awful bone-shattering thunk of impact, a child's screams, the door flying open, my body rolled in a tight ball, bouncing high in the long, thick grass, into darkness.

* * *

Forward he went, right through the windshield, I heard in the back of the ambulance. Mr. Luce was bloodied and unconscious. On the road was a small body, covered with a sheet.

9

I SURVIVED THE ACCIDENT with a sprained shoulder and a
broken arm. My mother came to the hospital to take me
home. "You're alive, that's all that counts," she said, because
she didn't realize at that moment what Mr. Luce had done. It
didn't strike her as problematic that I was in the truck with
him, just unfortunate that the accident had happened.

Yet I felt myself overcome by a deep and abiding sense of
shame. It was skin that grew tight to my bones, this shame. I
felt that the accident was my fault. I'd been happy when Mr.
Luce offered me a ride, he was going to be my special friend,
we would have meaningful conversations. Good luck. My
presence encouraged him to talk, the way cab drivers in the
city sometimes tell personal stories to strangers they will never
see again. If I hadn't been there, nothing would have distracted
him from watching the road. Fear and remorse ground its way
into my stomach. It made me feel like throwing up.

"Someone pulled out in front of him," my mother told me.
"That's what the police say."

"I saw the car."

"They need to put a stoplight there." She held my hand.

I was afraid to ask about Mr. Luce. Or the child.

"Your dad's been screaming about that turn for years."

A policeman came in and asked me a few questions: where
I'd been going with Mr. Luce, what I'd seen and remembered

of the accident. I told him Mr. Luce was a neighbour, that he was giving me a lift to my Summer Ed class at Linden High, that I saw the car shoot across the truck's path, that Mr. Luce swerved to avoid him, then jumped the curb. I mentioned seeing a child at the bus stop.

"The child is in critical condition," the officer said.

I felt sick. *I'm going to get arrested*, I thought.

He was silent for a moment. "I'll call your school," he said at last. "So they'll know you're safe."

He patted my good shoulder. I wept.

* * *

I didn't dare ask about Mr. Luce.

My mother used to be a nurse, so she took me in hand, driving me home and helping me upstairs to my room. On that hot July day, I was shivering under a blanket. Drifting off to sleep, I heard occasional sounds — my mother on the phone talking to my dad, then to neighbours. I slept, then woke and came downstairs in a daze. Trouble clouded the house; the air was thick with it, as if in moments the sky would turn green, then dark with a twister's fury. My mother looked grieved. She told me to rest on the screened porch where I'd catch a breeze. I stretched out on the chaise lounge and flipped through the pages of Jean Kerr's *Please Don't Eat The Daisies*. It had zero intellectual heft, which was fine. It was my mother's book, and I wanted to stay close to her.

I started reading, until I became aware of a murmur in the house, one that grew in intensity as if bees were circling a hive. Betty-Ann was home from work, and then I heard my mother's voice. *Claire's out on the porch, she's in shock, just be* — My mother's sentence drifted off as she followed my sister. Betty-Ann strode up to me.

"I can't believe this," she said.

"I was in an accident."

"You saw Loo-chay kill Todd Miller!"

It was the first I'd heard that Todd was dead. I fainted.

Mom grabbed cold towels and smelling salts. My eyes blinked open.

I guess I was getting too much attention. My sister started to bawl.

My dad came out on the porch and turned to Betty-Ann.

"And who do you think cut Mr. Luce off?" he asked. "Your idiot boyfriend, Don Wheeler."

"That's a lie. Claire got Loo-chay hot and bothered till he couldn't see straight."

I wanted to punch her, but my arm was in a sling.

"That is *vulgar*," said mom.

"You always take her side," said Betty-Ann, and her eyes welled up with tears.

Poor Todd. Poor Gracie. Poor Mr. Luce. I wanted to cry, but tears felt like something that didn't belong to me. Betty-Ann always had a hammer-lock on big emotion, always seeming to get to it first and snatching it out of my hands. This time she monopolized grief and filled the room with sobs. It was as if she'd gone behind my eyes and stolen my tears.

"Will you all stop it please," said my mother. "It's suppertime."

"It's a fact, what I'm saying," said my father.

"Justice will be done," Mom whispered.

"Like hell it will," said Dad. "Don Wheeler's the mayor's son."

10

M R. LUCE SUFFERED LACERATIONS, whiplash, a fractured sternum. He was going too fast to stop on a dime, said the police. Young Don Wheeler had been going even faster, didn't even stop. Neighbours said the cops were sorry to have to charge a law-abiding man for speeding down Rose Hill Road, since it was everyone's bad habit. Except that he'd killed a child, and they had no choice. Everyone in town felt troubled, alert to the fact that it could have happened to any one of them. Few wanted to say it was Mr. Luce's fault. *You think maybe now we'll get a Yield sign?* they asked. *They should go after the Parks Department, and fine the guy who looks after these woods.*

He'd been speeding, I knew that.

My parents said Mr. Luce was desolate. He wouldn't leave the house, my dad told Mom. He couldn't face the Millers next door. I wondered about poor Grace. Todd had been her only friend on the street, and she must be feeling devastated. Then I remembered her dad's eerie painting of Todd, how the boy's face showed contempt for him, as if he'd understood his own fate. I felt unnerved. Maybe Mr. Luce was insane. If so, then the fact that I'd cared so much about him meant I was crazy, too. I pondered this, feeling ashamed. By wanting to be a friend to Mr. Luce, I'd let something show, some ugly part of me that crouched behind my polite and studious manner. Now he had gone and killed someone. I felt that I was supposed to avoid him, and yet I couldn't buy into my sister's cruelty.

I told you he was a creep, she said. *I was right, wasn't I?*

I wasn't sure what to do. *He's drinking too much*, I heard my mother whisper. *Poor soul.*

Mom asked me if I'd spoken to Grace. The Luces lived five blocks away, and it was easy for me to avoid them. By then, it had been a month since the accident and I'd forgotten about Grace's summer school class, her troubles with math. In truth, I was afraid of running into Mr. Luce, but mom pointed out that Grace, who loved both her dad and Todd, had to be in much worse shape than I was.

The next day, I made my way over to Grace's house and found her in the back yard, by her father's shed. She gave me a hard stare, her eyes fixed on my plaster cast.

"Can I sign it?" she asked.

"Sure."

I held out my arm. She took her black felt marker and wrote REMEMBER TODD MILLER in big, bold letters. "In case you forget," she said.

I felt branded. As if she were punishing me for riding with her dad. You could see her inscription from across the street.

"I write it everywhere," she said.

"You don't think we'll remember him?"

"I painted it on my dad's truck."

"Now that's mean."

"He doesn't care. He's not allowed to drive anymore."

"Even so, he —"

"You've got it bad for my dad, and Mr. Miller's got his hand up Mom's skirt. I heard —"

"Grace, that's not funny."

"You and my mother are sluts."

44

"You take that back. Your dad offered me a ride that day, that's all."

Grace paused. "Well — okay. My mom, at any rate. She and Mr. Miller. Carrying on for a year now, right underneath my window when the weather's nice. They think I'm deaf."

"Gracie, are you sure?"

"Moaning and groaning. That's no tomcat howl."

Back then, you never heard kids talk like that. I felt embarrassed.

Grace told me her mom wasn't sleeping in the same room as her dad. He wasn't feeling well and needed to be in his own bed, said her mom. *Remember when you were sick last summer?* she'd asked. *How much you enjoyed those cool sheets, a quiet room with the shades drawn. Dad needs that for a while.* Her father was sick, and she heard the word *melancholy,* and she knew it meant sad. Her dad had the disease of sadness.

"He's sad because of Todd?" I asked.

"My mother's a liar. I hate them both. She fucks Mr. Miller twice a day."

"*Gracie.*"

"So make me shut up. Go on."

I was stunned because I couldn't, but also because I felt some excitement in watching Grace tighten all the faucets, shutting off the last drip-drip of childhood. A quick twist and the sparkling water's gone, the tap's dry, and she's hardening like jiffy-cement. I could see it happening, right that very minute. A sewer was backing up and flooding her mind with thoughts that should have made her ashamed. She was a threatening little brat, breaking rules, saying things I'd never dare to say, strutting around, swinging her hips. I could just picture her in years to come, hair dyed peroxide blonde, eyes thick with mascara, a tighter-than-tight skirt, a cigarette dangling from her mouth.

"When I grow up, I'll make my living on the street," she said.

"And where'll that get you?"

"Rich," she said. "I'll buy a gun and kill my parents."

"It'll get you in jail. Look, Gracie — "

"Oh, my God." Straight ahead was her father, headed for the shed.

Neither of us wanted to see him.

"Let's hide," said Grace. She grabbed my hand, and we headed down the back slope, hidden by a boulder and a small grove of trees that edged their way into a ravine. She pulled me to the ground behind the rock, then pointed to a tree half-overturned, its giant roots forming a kind of cave.

"I used to play in there with Todd," she whispered. She sounded more like a kid again. "Wanna go have a look?" Her eyes were hard and bright as moons. "I'll take off all my clothes and you can touch me."

"I'm going home now."

"Scaredy-cat."

I jumped up and ran.

* * *

When we were children, the two of them would drift through another reality, Todd lost in some meandering sunbeam of a thought, Grace dissolving into I-have-forever as she observed a ladybug crawling across her hand. The pair had lived in a separate place where every moment existed at once, a great eternal net cast across the sparkling waters of sense and thought. Unsorted, unfiled, clockless, Grace stroking the sunlit filaments of baby Todd's hair, pressing her nose into the golden florets of a daisy, getting Todd to do the same, to bloom, whole and entire. Now Grace had suffered the first of all bereavements. She has lost eternity and fallen into the prison of time. She can no longer float with Todd through the moment of death and out the other side, her hand stroking Todd's hair, the boys at day-camp waiting for him with a ball and catcher's mitt. Lost forever, the only heaven there was, but she'd discovered that she, too, was mortal, that mortal flesh offered its own consolations. She had learned from her mother's loneliness.

Touch me.

* * *

"Did you see Grace?" my mother asked.

"And how," I said. I showed her the graffiti on my plaster cast.

"Never mind," my mother said. "It's coming off next week."

11

THAT EVENING, MY FATHER went to visit Mr. Luce. He came home with a sealed envelope that he handed to me. I opened it.

Dear Claire,

I am writing to express my sincere apologies for having injured you in the truck on the morning of July 7th. If I could do it again, it would all be different, and you and young Todd would be safe. Only try as we might, we can't go back and change the wrong we do. I have told your parents that I will pay for your medical costs. I hope you will recover soon. All I can do is ask your forgiveness.

Sincerely,

Mr. A. Luce

I showed the letter to my parents.

"Guy's got a conscience, at least," Dad said.

I knew he was thinking about money. My medical expenses were covered by insurance, but I would have to see a physiotherapist, which was expensive.

"You've spoken to Grace?" mom asked.

I hesitated. "Yeah, and she's really upset," I said.

"You were very nice to talk to her."

"But I don't know how to help her."

"You do," said Mom. "Just be her friend."

I wasn't sure how to do that, either.

* * *

I took Mr. Luce's letter upstairs to my room and read it over and over. *Only try as we might, we can't go back and change the wrong we do.* His words of contrition rested in my heart. *All I can do is ask your forgiveness.* I'd wanted to talk about art and politics and the Big World, but our friendship would begin with his depth of honesty. To acknowledge it, I would have to say *I forgive you,* but I was too shy. *It wasn't even your fault,* I thought, but then I thought again. There was Todd's lost life to think about. Mr. Luce had done that. *Guy's got a conscience, at least,* said Dad. Not like Don Wheeler, speeding down the road. According to Dad, he hadn't apologized to anyone.

Never mind, I told myself. *One day there will be justice. One day I'll be friends with Mr. Luce.*

I believed that.

* * *

"Mr. Luce's sick," my mother said to me a week later. "He had to go to the hospital."

"What's wrong with him?" I asked.

"He's — very sad," she said.

I puzzled over that one. There were lots of sad people out there, none of them in hospital beds. There were lots more questions, too, none of which I'd get answered. When I asked who would look after Grace, Mom told me she'd live with her mother. She refused to discuss the fact that Nora Luce, now pregnant, had left her husband and was living as Lyle Miller's wife. After Todd's death, Mrs. Miller had gone home to England and had not returned, but she didn't talk about that either.

"Is he — depressed?" I asked.

"Claire." The sound of my name slammed like a door. "Let's drop this."

Betty-Ann had just walked into the room.

"He's a mental case, so they're giving him shock treatments," she said. "Afterwards, he'll be a vegetable."

I got busy setting the table for dinner.

"Why do you always exaggerate?" my mother asked.

"I'm not. Nora told me for a fact. It's true."

"Then it's nothing to smile about," said Mom.

* * *

Betty-Ann was upset, I knew that, even as she commuted to the city for her summer job at Chanel, musing over her dreams for the future. In the fall she'd begin college, and she'd hoped her engagement to Don would follow soon after. Yet her boyfriend was withdrawn these days, wasn't spending time with her, and because of this, she felt certain that I'd derailed her plans by distracting Mr. Luce and setting off an ugly rockslide of destruction. With Betty-Ann, it always happened that her soul would sizzle and fry on a burner of pain and disappointment, then flip right over into a heaping mess of sarcasm and cruelty. Betty-Ann could never just be sad.

After her snide remarks about Mr. Luce's mental state, she started to pick away at me as if I were an ugly zit on perfect skin. In fact, I was as close as she could get to Mr. Luce and to the grossness of his moral imperfection. I reminded her of him, can you believe it? I had nobody-genes, dark like his. I could converse with him in my dreary, nobody way. I shared his nobody taste in art. *You even look like him,* she said once.

I glanced in the mirror when she wasn't there. Dark hair. Dark eyes. Then the truth hit me.

"You're the one who's obsessed with him," I said to her.

"With that greaser? Not my style."

"Then why do you bring him up, every chance you get?"

After that, she didn't bug me as much.

Yet I wondered what my sister thought of Don Wheeler's role in the tragedy.

He and Betty-Ann had been sweethearts long before the accident, and now he was in active duty in the Armed Forces Reserves. He told her it was time well spent because it gave him a chance to think. He had lots to mull over, having been in trouble with the law, his foot on the gas, his brain in outer space. He'd been charged with careless driving and put on probation. He got a speeding ticket.

"Would of been worse if he wasn't the mayor's kid," said Dad.

"It was Mr. Luce's fault," said Betty-Ann.

"Like hell it was. I'm getting a half-wit as a son-in-law," Dad snapped.

"Only if Claire marries Mr. Luce."

You see what I mean? After the accident, Betty-Ann just said things and got away with it, like a sniper on a building letting loose. Nimble with words, I lobbed a few right back at her. *Self-defence*, I told myself, since I knew my parents felt as helpless as I did. They tossed out a few timid objections during these verbal firefights, as if they knew my sister needed something in the way of confrontation, something they hadn't the stamina to provide. For reasons unknown to me, Betty-Ann was frantic to build a home of human timber, to disassemble her family limb from limb as if we were there to warm her, nothing more.

12

DON WHEELER'S DAD was a three-term mayor and a card-carrying Legionnaire, his wife a Daughter of the American Revolution, one of those DAR *hausfraus* convinced there were wood-eating commies in the floorboards. Thanks to the Wheelers, Betty-Ann and I spent our childhoods crouching under desks, practicing what we'd do in the event of an enemy attack. Mrs. Wheeler got the whole thing organized, all the duck-and-cover flyers and propaganda films, her and her chum Mrs. Luce, now Mrs. Miller. Even as a little kid, I found these air raid drills incongruous. *The roof could cave in,* I thought. *The floor-to-ceiling windows would shatter from the force of the blast.* We could hide in a basement, only then the building might collapse and grate us up like parmesan cheese.

"Don't worry, it'll never happen," said Dad when I asked him. "We've got a strong deterrent, honey, that's the key."

All of which brings me to my story.

Three years had passed since the accident. I'd seen Mr. Luce from time to time, driving a truck into town. He'd appealed to get his driver's license back so that he could work for a house-painting company. He didn't live in Linden anymore. I was dating a guy on the debate team at a nearby boys' school, nothing serious, just some fun, and I'd started applying to colleges. Yet I hadn't forgotten that man. He haunted me, a lonely piece of life's story, a sentence with no punctuation, no proper end. I had no idea that in real life, people often drift away from us, and their stories meander downhill in no particular direction. I felt certain that somehow, we'd reconnect.

We did, but in the strangest of ways.

We had spring and fall air raid drills. That April, the sirens whined their steady run-for-cover as our senior class 12-A filed into the school's library. "A safe room, no windows," said Sister Agnes. "Double-reinforced walls as strong as steel."

I crouched under a table and gave it some thought.

Reinforced with what? With words, ideas. It was a library, after all.

In the event of an enemy attack, read a good book to help pass the time, I thought. There were worse ways to die than under a heap of Milton and Shakespeare. There was even a precedent for this. A short work by John Hersey on the survivors of Hiroshima described the trauma of one Miss Sasaki: "In the first moment of the atomic age, a human being was crushed by books."

Well, now.

Squatting under a long table with three other girls, I turned toward the bookshelves and eyed the bottom row of dusty tomes. *Reading, what a way to go.* I reached out and pulled a book off the shelf. It was a slim volume, the same blue colour as our uniforms. *A Stillness on the Earth,* the poetry of one Alison Lange, published ten years earlier, in 1953. *For my son,* the dedication read.

I should have seen this coming.

The night's a conjurer's box.
I lift the lid, observe its emptiness.
No moon, no light.

Reaching in I pull out silence,

touching the ash of stars,
a man's remains.

I kept reading. I found myself lost in the bone-cold chill of it, the feel of the paper, the careful and elegant printing of the words. It may not have been great writing but it was modern verse, words trotting and dancing across the page like colts out of harness, and I loved its freedom. Alison Lange wrote about space, and her photo showed a woman with the fine, quiet gaze of one who carried it inside her. *She writes about life in northern Canada,* said the note on the back, *speaking larger truths with lyricism and wisdom.*

I'd only ever met one guy from Canada.

The long blast of the siren continued and I slipped the book in my pocket. *A good simulation,* I thought. *In a real air raid, there wouldn't be time to sign it out.* Moments later the all-clear sounded and we filed back into our classes.

* * *

What sad connections that little book made. The previous fall, there'd been an air raid drill during the Cuban Missile Crisis when the whole school marched across the yard and down to the church basement. The older students had to line up next to the kindergarten and first grade kids. Bundled-up little tots shuffled in next to us, tiny confused silences, a long row of them. It sickened me, that they'd do this to children. Maybe next time, I'd refuse to take part. Imagine, a straight-A student, a class monitor lying down in front of the school in protest. What a bad example for the little kids. I'd get expelled.

I wasn't the first to think of it, however.

As a monitor, I had to herd the younger kids back to class after the all-clear, making sure none of the smaller ones wandered off. On alert for miscreants, I entered the narrow passageway between the school and the church. Up ahead was a garbage pail, its lid moving with a suspicious clank. This was something new. Even gas from rotting lunches couldn't give it a push like that.

Out came Grace Luce, and she was sobbing.

"Gracie!"

She slumped down against the wall, her eyes stricken. There were bruises on her arms.

"You hurt yourself?"

"Fell," she said.

"In the garbage pail?" She nodded.

"I won't tell," I said. "It's okay."

"I want to die." She started to cry again.

"Gracie, no."

I held her and it felt as if I were embracing misery itself, a bundled heap of sorrow, Grace who'd turned into one of those kids who was always getting in trouble with the nuns, who "didn't work up to her capacity" (as Sister Agnes said), a loner who survived only because her vast and stormy paintings were good enough to win trophies. Right then she scared me. I'd never met anyone who wanted to die.

"Gracie, I'd miss you," I said.

She looked away. "I won't miss anyone," she replied. "If we ever have a real air raid, I'll kill myself."

"You're *morbid*."

Her eyes were sizzling like hot oil, smoking mad as she glared at me.

"When they drop the Bomb, you puke up your guts and you *die*," she said. "It takes *hours*."

You've got a point there, Gracie, I thought. I walked her back to class.

Poor, bruised kid, that was no garbage pail that clunked her. At the end of the term, her mother and Mr. Miller sent her off to a boarding school upstate. A strict shape-em-up place for problem kids whose rich parents hoped to avoid future court dates and bad publicity. *Rock-Smashing 101,* said Betty-Ann with a smirk.

In Alison Lange's book was a poem called "Desolate Child." I gazed at the author's photo, and I saw Grace's eyes emerging in her face. I knew then who the poet was.

13

W HEN I ARRIVED HOME, Betty-Ann was sitting at the kitchen table doing her nails, with *Modern Bride* open in front of her. She was a college junior now, commuting to the city, living at home to be close to Don. She looked up when I walked in, the book sticking out of my pocket.

"What's that you've got?" she asked.

"Poems," I said. "By Alison Lange."

She frowned. "Who?"

"Alison Lange."

"Never heard of her."

"A friend of Jackie Kennedy's."

She snatched the book out of my pocket, scrutinizing the photo on the back. "What awful hair. She's no friend of Jackie."

I shrugged.

"All of which reminds me — you'll do something about your hair for the wedding, hon?"

"When are you getting married?"

"We're booking the club for a year this June."

"So next year I'll get it done," I said.

"Sweetie, get it done well ahead. You'd look so pretty with a bouffant style."

I hated it when she called me sweetie.

"All the bridesmaids' dresses will be pink petal-layered chiffon," she continued, "except for the maid of honour in deep rose, and you'll all have rose bouquets. June and roses just naturally go together."

"Too subtle," I said.

She was still talking when I went to my room.

It might have been the uncertainty of her impending marriage that was causing her anxiety. Don was stationed at a base in Virginia. There was no formal engagement, no wedding date, nothing but the charred smell of imagination landing on a hidden third rail running through her brain, making horrible sizzling noises as she spoke. On top of that, Betty-Ann couldn't stop talking. She'd gotten into the habit of offloading drivel, unlocking her brain, tipping it backwards into her listener's head like the rear of a massive dump-truck into a landfill. I doubt my sister meant that to happen, not at such intensity. Left out of her monologues were things that might have drawn me into the conversation. Only what I said never mattered.

"Betty-Ann should see a psychiatrist," I'd said to Mom a few weeks earlier.

She'd looked shocked. "What for?"

"Because she doesn't live in the real world."

"Are you so perfect?" said my mother.

Grownups knew nothing.

I sat in my room, reading the jacket of Alison Lange's book. "She had to deal with madness," said the blurb. That afternoon, I'd been crouching on my hands and knees, head down, finding respite in a book I'd stolen, as if the bombs were already falling and law had vanished. I checked the radio clock, six p.m.

Crazy-time.

Forgetting Betty-Ann, I stared at a worse kind of madness: the station-band embossed with icons of civil defence. Even the Top Forty came packaged with a sense of dread there was no escaping. Two frequencies were marked by small triangulated circles: six-forty, twelve-forty, CONELRAD, Control of Electromagnetic Radiation. When atomic bombs started dropping, all but those two stations would go off the air, assuming there were any still on the air. Odds were they'd notice a brilliant flash of light — their feet transparent, the bones visible, like those kiddie shoe-fitting X-ray machines of years ago that hit 'em with a full-body dose. Atomic shoes, red-hot feet, *shake it up baby, twist and shout.* Bulletins would dangle from the shredded remains of America's broadcast system, from two stations at either end of the dial: *Take shelter immediately. This is not a test.*

My family knew how I hated that stuff.

Alison Lange was a talisman, the missing piece that held together all these broken recollections. *I found your book during an air raid drill and that was how you spoke to me.* I had to write and tell her this, sure she'd make sense of my confusion. She was a poet, and poetry was connection, the current from the plug that lit the light. *This* was like *that.* Everything. *Shall I compare you to a summer's day?* Or to your lost grandchild, made suicidal by the dread of war? (Or, more to the point, by the bruises on her arms.)

Mr. Luce's mother, Grace's grandmother — somehow I convinced myself that Alison could help me. I kept a diary then, a big, brave notebook without a lock and key. In it I wrote: *No child will ever despair, never again. I am going to find Alison Lange. I am going to take the radio apart and remove the* CONELRAD *markings. I am going to take apart every goddamn radio in America and pry loose these monograms of death.*

At last I had a goal in life, something I could talk about with as much ferocity as Betty-Ann. Energized, I strode downstairs to supper.

"We had to take part in the drill," said Dad as he buttered a slab of bread.

"Where'd they put you?" I asked.

"Basement," he said. "Lead and concrete. Double-reinforced."

"We were in the library," I told him. "Books. Double-reinforced."

"Doesn't matter where you're put," said Dad. "They'll never attack."

"You're not scared?" I asked.

"Idea's to show 'em we mean business, hon. That's all."

"Have some more clam chowder," Mom said.

Betty-Ann glanced at me and cleared her throat. "Some people got arrested in Central Park," she said. "They wouldn't take part. All long-hair pacifist types."

"Soup's great, Mom," I said.

"One thing about pacifists is that they're cowards. They never speak up."

I took a deep breath. "Bertrand Russell speaks up," I told her.

"He's an atheist," said Betty-Ann.

"Mrs. Roosevelt goes to church. She speaks up."

"That ugly old bag." Betty-Ann turned to mom. "Claire thinks pink like Mrs. Roosevelt. I read it in her diary."

"You read my *diary*?"

"Mrs. Roosevelt has facial hair," said Betty-Ann.

"You have the brains of a clam." I picked up my bowl of chowder and threw it in Betty-Ann's face.

Mom sent me to my room. Downstairs, I heard her voice. *Betty-Ann, why do you have to provoke your sister?*

The TV clicked on and Dad watched the news.

Later that evening Mom came upstairs and gave me the key to my room. "Protect yourself," she said.

Why don't you protect me?

Madness, I realized, was a disease you could catch.

Alone in my room, I unplugged my radio, took my letter opener and pried loose the clear plastic frame that protected the frequency band. *Shit, those goddamn things are printed on.* I went into the bathroom, retrieved Betty-Ann's bright red nail polish, inked out the circles and replaced the plastic frame. I hummed a few bars of *Oh, Freedom*, and went to sleep with the radio on.

14

ALISON LANGE ANSWERED my letter, enclosed directions to her house and invited me to visit her in Connecticut. An easy trip — just four stops away on the New Haven train, so I rode my bike to Linden station, feeling adult and independent, on a quest of my own. It was a trip I'd announced to my parents, who were glad I'd take a break from studying for finals. When I arrived, I realized that Alison's lovely old home felt familiar in a disconcerting way. I wasn't sure why until I noticed a ladder propped against the side of the house, and then I understood why I'd come here. *You'll have a chance to meet my son,* said Alison's note. It had been a long time since I'd spoken to the man in work clothes climbing down the ladder, for years the object of my inner conversations, my musings on the world. Mr. Luce turned around. His thick black hair was tinged with silver, and his lost weight made him seem bereaved. Even so, he still had a strong, remarkable presence. I said hello.

He smiled, extending his hand. "Claire, is it?"

I couldn't remember. My hands were damp.

"Nice to see you," I said.

"And you."

My nerves were crackling like radio static when a storm's approaching. Anything could happen. Any embarrassing thing might slip out of my mouth. I ran up the porch steps and rang the bell.

Alison opened the door and welcomed me. She was a slight woman with brilliant blue eyes and cloud-like skin. There was an odd translucence about her as if she were made of light-enhancing substances: silks, opals, rain. I felt as if she were a curtain and that if I were to draw her open, I'd float through her and into the sky.

We sat down and without preamble, she began to tell me about her late husband Tom, who long ago came home ill from working in the uranium mines in Canada's far northwest. Two years after the man's death, Alison packed what few things she had, taking her son far away with her to New York City, to marriage with a man who loved her. He was a wealthy American, a mine-owner who'd met her in Canada on business, a good but distant man. So they'd lived well, thank God, but the loss of the north was an ache in Alastair's heart, and until he met Nora, he was unconsoled. Even then, in his own home on Long Island Sound, he'd recall his father and feel as lost.

"I didn't know about his father," I said.

She got up and found a book that she handed to me. It was, she explained, a fictional memoir based on this period of her life. In her sitting room, the walls were old with photos, and she pointed to one of Tom, her first husband. He looked much like Mr. Luce. Then she handed me a photo of her son with a small girl. Grace.

"How can you help her?" she asked me.

I was startled by the question. Here I'd hoped to sort out my confusion and Alison had identified the only way I could. I told her about the day I found Grace in the alleyway, and how worried I'd been. She showed me one of her granddaughter's paintings, a wild abstraction of a tormented face, its mood at war with its brilliant, sun-like gold. A few months after she'd painted it, she covered a school wall with ochre paint and got herself suspended.

I remembered her paint-job on Mr. Miller's fence and her dad's laconic reaction. "Art runs in your family," I said.

"You know her father, is that it?"

"Not at all well," I said. I stammered, then told Alison I was sorry he'd been ill.

"He is so much like his own father," she replied.

I told her I was riding with him, the day of the accident.

"So it was you," she said.

I finished her sentence. *Who distracted him. Who caused him to swerve and kill that child.*

"How ashamed he was, that he hurt you."

I told her he'd written, asking forgiveness.

Alison never took her eyes off me. As I told her what had happened, she listened in the same way that she spoke, with absolute assurance and conviction. She made me think of a radio astronomer trying to interpret a vast array of data from the stars, mindful of the fact that her ears moved beyond sound into sight while her eyes saw so much that the vast, unseeable light of things broke through into a kind of music. There was also wariness in her, as if she understood the value of her way of knowing, its difference from the world's. At last she spoke.

"Many people step around Alastair."

"Why?"

"Alcohol. Mental illness." She paused. "Those things don't bother you?"

"He was very kind to me," I replied.

"And you liked him."

"I liked having a grown-up friend."

"He's had electroshock," his mother said.

Alison took pains to tell me that the Mr. Luce I knew no longer existed. Gone was the odd light of his paintings, the way in which he was different from the rest of us. In his place was a docile, cooperative man.

"It was a mercy," said Alison. "He suffered too much. But this mustn't happen to my grandchild."

I was troubled to think it might.

"Will you be a friend to Grace?"

Her voice felt like an engraver's tool, and my heart like glass. I told her I already was.

"All that talent. Will you help her?"

I said I'd do my best.

She put the kettle on for tea, then went outside to get Mr. Luce. I shivered as I glanced around the room, at its assortment of china and cut glass. I felt as frail as these things — wan, transparent, light as air and as empty, possessed by memories and dreams that weren't mine. Each object carried its own sadness, an expression of some moment that I'd never understand, the brittle reality of grief and unlived lives. Yet as I pondered this, I found it impossible to believe that Mr. Luce as I'd known him had vanished beyond my reach. I went to a window that looked out on Alison's garden, her dogwoods and cherry trees in flower. He must have grown with these trees, and were he to touch the roughness of their bark or the softness of their flowers, the past would return. He remembered my name. Under the window stood a small table covered with a piece of crocheted needlework. On it was a silver box.

I opened it. In its cluster of antique jewellery, I noticed a plain gold ring. It must have been Alison's wedding band, with *1921* engraved on the inside, along with the inscription, *A. & T.L.* I picked it up. In my hand I sensed a closed circle of forgotten hopes, and I recalled the books in Mr. Luce's basement, how burdened they felt with lost dreams, with their immensity of longing.

A man's eyes glanced at me through the window.

I put the ring down and walked away from the table. Outside I could hear the rough sounds of Mr. Luce at work, the back door slamming, boot-steps in the hall, the splash of water. He seemed shy in his mother's sitting room, uneasy as he glanced around. Alison returned and served us tea.

"I can give you a lift back," he said to me.

I hesitated, but only for a moment.

15

ALONE IN THE TRUCK with him, I felt shy. Worse, I felt I should have turned down the offer. The last time I'd sat in a truck with Mr. Luce, I'd been thrown out the door, ending up with broken bones and months of physio. If anything happened this time, I'd have no excuse. It would be my own fault. My parents would kill me if they found out I'd taken this ride. I fell silent.

"Your family well?" he asked me.

"Fine," I said.

"Yourself?"

"I'm off to college in the fall." I asked him how business was.

"Can't complain."

I'd heard he'd lived for a while with his mother. Dad told Mom he was better now, that he'd found an apartment in the town of Beaches Point. *Poor soul*, Mom said out of Betty-Ann's earshot, but Dad reassured Mom that Mr. Luce was no such thing. He was getting back on his feet, a hard worker, not some welfare leech. Alcoholism and mental illness were diseases, said my dad. Like polio. As with that sickness, Dad was convinced that one day American medical know-how would come to the rescue, would lick whatever ailed poor Mr. Luce.

At least they were kind, my parents. I waited for a stoplight, then glanced at the man beside me. *Here goes*, I thought.

"Do you still paint pictures, Mr. Luce?" I asked.

"Alastair."

"Alastair," I said. "Do you —"

"It's been a while."

I remembered his self-portrait that used to hang in his living room, a taciturn, muscular, square-jawed man with thick black hair, sturdy in a way that didn't match the shyness of his glance. It wasn't something I'd let on to Betty-Ann, that his paintings revealed to me his solemnity and depth. To my eye, they were rough ore, rich with precious lodes of memory. It was around the time when Grace first showed me his work that I noticed in her living room a painting of a wintry scene, a picket line, black-clad labourers, placards reading *On Strike*. I thought of a matchbook, *close cover before striking*, feeling the heat of a row of faces set to burn. *Where?* I asked her dad.

"Winnipeg," he told me. "The general strike of 1919."

"Where's Winnipeg?"

"Manitoba, Canada," he said.

"Is it very cold?"

He paused. "In winter, yes. All of Canada's cold then."

He'd said that with tenderness, as if he were recalling some lost joy, and I was moved as if the memory were my own. More than this, I'd felt as if he'd welcomed me into the silence of his homeland. No doubt he'd also revealed this abode of peace to Grace. Remembering this, I told Alastair that she'd be an artist someday, that she'd pick up where he left off.

"You think so?"

"She takes after you."

Alastair's hands gripped the wheel. The light changed. He drove in silence. At the next stoplight, he spoke. "She's just run away," he said.

"Run away where?"

"Canada."

By then I knew that Canada was a pretty huge place. Just the name raised more questions than I could ask before the light turned green. "How come?" was all I could manage.

"Didn't like school, I guess."

I remembered that after her parents' divorce, Grace had wanted to live with her dad, but the court said no. Running off to his native land was pure Grace, middle finger straight up. Alastair told me that she'd called him yesterday, and that was the first he'd heard of it. He hadn't told his mother yet.

"It's my job to worry," he said. "Not hers."

I worried too. Back in the sixties, it wasn't cheap to call long distance. I wondered where Grace got the money. I asked him if he knew where she was. He told me she was staying at a rooming house in Toronto, owned by a retired teacher, an old friend of his mother's. The woman, a Mrs. Wells, had once come down to visit and left her address.

"The Millers put her in boarding school," he said. "Too strict for her."

"Are you going to Toronto?"

"Yes," he said, his voice quiet.

We drove in silence. At the next light, I asked him when he was leaving.

"Very soon," he said.

"I'm going away to college soon. In two months."

"Be back before that," he said.

"My sister can't wait for me to clear out."

Stopping for a red light, he gazed ahead, then spoke as if I weren't there.

"Families live alone," he said.

I felt the silence in the words.

* * *

In the quiet that followed, I remembered the day of the accident, how a policeman came over to speak to Dad. *Kid in the car cut off Al Luce*, the cop said. *Helluva grade, Al was rolling right downhill, hit the brake, must of lost control.* On the front page of the paper was a photo of Don Wheeler. *Everyone knows who did it,* said Betty-Ann later, but Dad told her to leave it to the judge.

Betty-Ann said nothing to me. When she was alone, she took the newspaper and with her long fingernails began shredding the front-page story. She wept in silence, and then the tears stopped and the shredding turned deliberate, becoming a fringe, a few leaves, a flower. *For poor Todd*, she said to no one in particular. *Poor little boy, just waiting for the bus.* She began slicing and twisting the rest of the paper with a rapid and terrible skill. *Dumb greaser.* Rip, shred, twist, turn.

* * *

"Families do what they want to do," said Alastair.

"They'll have to do it without me."

"I wish you happiness," he said.

The words shivered inside me.

As he spoke, I recalled Betty-Ann talking to Mom in the kitchen. It was a week or two ago, but I could still hear an edge of anger in her voice, a tight smile glazed with reproach that signalled me to stay away, that curdled my own tongue with nasty comebacks. There won't be a rock on her finger this season. Forget the wedding with the arch of swords — Don quit the reserves. He's told her he had to sort his life out, decide what he's going to do with himself. He planned to spend the summer with a work-group in Mexico, building roads and hospitals, improving his Spanish, teaching kids. He felt he'd been over-privileged, that he had to show repentance for the loss of Todd Miller, that he ought to prevent the deaths of innocent children, that he hoped to atone for a man's ruined life. There was the tart sting of unsaid words in the air, and my mother sensed them.

Mr. Luce has suffered enough, she said. My sister pulled out an emery board and got to work on her nails.

* * *

Yes, he's suffered enough. The thought moved me. Mr. Luce had no solace, no comfort. None at all.

He asked me how Betty-Ann was.

"She looked after Grace when things were rough," he said.

"Your friend Grace has turned into a first-class bitch," my sister had said a while back. "Stole a hundred bucks from Mr. Miller, went joy-riding with a sailor. Stone-drunk and under-age, too. She's got her parents worried sick, that's why they sent her away."

"Where'd they send her?"

"To a boot-camp school. One step away from the slammer."

"Folks have been kind," said Alastair. "You learn from that."

I told him yes, you learn.

* * *

Alastair pulled his truck into Linden Station. It was getting late, and I noticed that my bike was the only one left on the rack. I thanked him for the ride.

"I want to thank you, Claire," he said.

"For what?" I asked.

He took me in his arms, and held me as he stroked my hair.

"For your kindness," he said. "That you would even ride with me."

I told him I'd forgiven him.

"God bless you," he said.

I wanted to cry.

Then he let go of me. He promised to let me know how Grace was.

16

IT WAS ONLY WHEN I returned home that I remembered the slender book, the fictional tale his mother had given to me. In my room, I locked the door and began to read.

...As if he were drifting in and out of sleep, he's painting high above the town, he imagines an intensity of colour, he can feel his father's hard-working hands in his own. Lost inside the silence of memory, he sees a miner in the anguish of his final illness, a man who spoke with passion of light in the cleft of the rock, of a colour beyond what the eye can see. All his life, he'd feared what his father had suffered, but now he's trapped in the grip of pain like a fox in a leg-hold who can't free himself. To northern Ontario he returns in memory, to his childhood home in the bush outside of Sudbury, alive and fragrant with spruce and jack-pine, the chill beauty of a spring night under the moon, the snow as remote and vacant as a stare. His father, a good man in his fisherman's shack, sits drinking under the stars, alone. Oh moon, oh bitter earth, writes his mother. What hope is there?

There'd been hope when his father left us for country even more remote than this. The north seemed to stretch into an infinite distance, this compass direction so different from the others, the one that drew his father toward the far northwest, to a rock full of stars, the furthest sky. The boy was ten years

old *when his father left, yet he'd understood and wasn't angry,
imagining the man in parka and sealskin boots, and he'd hear
in his sleep the gentle tapping of his miner's pick, dreaming
the fissures his father made in the rock of Port Radium, how
they broke open to reveal the light within.* A luminous starry
thing, *his father wrote.* Even though you cannot see the stars.
They use it for medicine and for watches that glow in the night.
Can you tell the time yet, son? *He'd sent them money during
the Depression, when others had little to spend. More than
this, he'd sent them dreams, an unquenchable light. He had a
gift this way, his father, a knack for extraordinary visions. It
saved his family. He left the gift to his son.*

*Yet the young man drifts above the rooftops, and remember-
ing the chill north, he's fourteen again, his father still dying.
That singular loss was the frozen ground on which my son
walked, the ice underneath the surface of his life.* Your dad
could never sleep, *I told him.* He'd talk to himself about the
stars in the rock. He'd drink. He'd wander off. *He'd see his
father then, radiant and lit from inside. There was x-ray light
behind the dark ladder of his ribcage and his bones shone with
a dazzling iridescence.* It's energy, son, the same as lights the
stars. *He'd see the man on fire. Opening a mickey of rye, he'd
drink it down, feel the man burning in his throat as he drank.*

*How he'd wanted his father close, then followed him to the
fisherman's shack at night, a man who'd come home from the
mines so drunk, so sick. Once upon a timeless story with a
dreadful end, the boy let the dog bark, forgot to fill the scuttle
with coal, and he took a beating from a poor, sick man with
dead cells in the marrow of his bones. Now it seems as if he
were cursed by his own father on that day when another child
was lost, when his hands gripped the wheel, the world turning
around the axis of his grief.*

Looking out the window on a cold spring night, the boy

had seen his father drunk and skidding over lake ice, and he got out of bed, dressed and ran to the shore. It was too late to stop the shearing of a great floe breaking under the weight of his father's feet, a black mouth opening in the water, drowning him. The round moon floated like a blessing on his father's grave. Everything died then.

I was shaken. Imagination shaped the tale, but I understood its source. In my youth, these kind of revelations were not as common as they are now. Alison's audience would have been small, a coterie of academics and Greenwich Village artists who loved bold declarations meant to shock. Her storytelling chilled me.

Earlier that day, she'd described Alastair as a docile man, cured of his suffering. I wondered what he felt about this.

17

FOR DAYS I WAS HAUNTED by Alison's words, how they seemed to have moulded Alastair. He lived head bowed, eyes lowered, as if his life since the accident had been formed by the words themselves. I wondered if he'd read them, if he'd chosen to live in their shadow. How grieved was he, knowing he couldn't restore what he'd destroyed? *Would you let me hold you?* said his arms. *I wanted to thank you for your kindness, that you would even ride with me.* The poor man was grateful even for Betty-Ann's "friendship" with Grace. *People are kind. You learn from that*, as if he deserved nothing better than my sister's contempt.

Yet his fragility stirred my heart, and once again, I wanted to befriend him. I forgot about the fact that I'd be leaving for college in two months. At home, I busied myself with preparations for the fall. *Did you write Mrs. Lange a thank-you note?* my mother asked when I told her how much I'd enjoyed the visit. I did this, and days later, she replied. *It was a pleasure meeting you. Alastair's called from Toronto. He says he'd like to talk to you about Grace — a good thing, since it's much too complex for this letter. He's back a week Monday. He goes strolling at Beaches Point, so if you see him there on any early morning, he will discuss it with you.*

This information startled and pleased me at the same time. Alastair had realized he couldn't call me at home, couldn't write me a note, but he'd found a way to connect. He wanted to see me. Had to, almost. I hugged myself, shivering with pleasure.

* * *

On early summer mornings, I used to enjoy riding my bike along the Linden shore where it abuts Rye Beach. It was nothing that would have made my parents suspicious. Only now I was on the lookout for Alastair, until a week later, I saw him.

He wasn't strolling. He was setting up an easel, he was organizing brushes and paints, he was sitting down on a folding stool, his brush applied to the canvas. Alastair was painting. His mother was wrong — *Docile and obedient*, she'd said. *He's not the man you knew. Maybe I gave him hope*, I thought. No one believed he'd paint again. I thought of Betty-Ann. *He's a mental case, so they're giving him shock treatments. Afterwards, he'll be a vegetable.* Every last one of them had been wrong. Like the spring light that returns a bird to its nesting-place, he'd come back to the light of early morning, to a lost place inside himself. Alastair was alive, hungry for life, drawing beauty out of the world. It was, I felt certain, the triumph of life over death.

In awe of this, I allowed the days to roll by like breakers on the shore until one early morning I knew I was ready to approach him. By now I could sense that he was rooted in his work, that he would continue after I'd left. He looked up and smiled.

"Would you mind if I painted you?" he asked.

He wanted to capture me in this light, he said. Later we'd talk about Grace.

Only we didn't talk, not right away. For several early mornings, I sat for him in that secluded spot, lost in the attention that I craved. As the light shifted into day, he'd pack his canvas and easel in the truck and head off to work painting houses. I who'd wanted to awaken hope in him saw instead that he was breathing life into me, as if I existed only in his heart. Each night I dreamt that he was in my bed, and before dawn I hurried over to Beaches Point. It seemed a miracle that Alastair, who'd suffered so much, could reach out to touch me in this way. When the painting was done, he showed it to me, an abstract work, silvery-white, delicate with muted pinks, pearly like the inside of a seashell.

"It's you," he said. "Fresh as lake water, bright as rock."

"Thank you."

Alastair put his hands on my shoulders. I felt him wrapped in longing, as if he had the winter garment of the lonely north all over him, and I could taste its sorrow in his lips as they rested on mine, his tongue slipping into my mouth, his body rocking against me. Then he stepped back.

"I'm sorry," he said.

"It's all right."

"No. I shouldn't have."

It stirred me more, how frail he seemed, how he backed away from what he'd done. "Forgive me," he murmured, and I felt at that moment that I could have slept with him, could have used his confusion to satisfy myself. Only he went to the trunk, rummaged around the glove compartment, and pulled out something, a pine cone. He let me touch it.

"From my home forest," he said. "From the lake."

"Where you lost your father." I handed it back to him.

"You know about this," he said.

"I read your mother's book."

Alastair was silent.

"Did you mind her writing it?"

"It's the truth," he said.

"It's so sad."

He shrugged. "That's the truth for you."

"Did your father really —?"

"He was sick." He paused. "Yeah, he was — pretty free with his hands, you might say."

"How awful."

"We all mess up," he said. "I was the opposite. I let Grace do whatever she wanted. Nora took it out on her."

Beat her up, you mean.

"Soon as I left for work." He sighed. "Gracie kept it all inside. Hardened up."

I imagined a swallow, wings flapping, bricked up inside a wall.

* * *

In Toronto, Grace had gone to stay at Mrs. Wells' rooming house, but by the time Alastair arrived, she'd left. The woman, a kindly soul, had found her babysitting jobs, had offered to get her into school in the fall. Only Mrs. Wells asked Grace to leave when she fell in with a rough crowd, brought home booze, had a guy stay overnight. Apparently she later moved in with him and his cronies in a flat over a convenience store on Dupont Street, and when her dad went to find her, he learned she'd stolen fifty bucks and fled.

Alastair didn't want to call the police. He tried the Y. Mrs. Wells had given him her number, asking him to call if he had no luck. He bought the *Tely* and the *Toronto Star*, and scanned them for articles on troubled kids. He thought about putting an ad in the paper. *Grace, your dad was here.* When he called Mrs. Wells, he learned that Grace had written to her. She'd received a note that she read to him over the phone. *I've decided to go back to the USA,* she wrote, *to my old school. When I straighten out, I'll come back. Next time don't be nice to a shit. You get more shit for your trouble.*

"You'll pardon my language," said Mrs. Wells.

"I apologize," said Alastair.

"She stole my gold watch."

* * *

"This is how life pays you back," said Alastair.

"No," I insisted. "Grace is responsible for her own actions."

"She learned it from me. I let her get away with things."

I remembered the painting episode, on Lyle Miller's back fence.

"Is she back at school?" I asked.

"She is." He paused. "It's like a jail, that school. I'm not allowed to visit her."

"You're not?"

"Court order. Nora saw to it."

Days passed, years went by in seconds, the clock's hands spinning backwards. Over and over I left for home and returned. Shadows fell into late afternoon, then dusk. I listened.

"I wanted to paint you," he said, "because of a thing I lost."

"What was that?"

"The painting I was making — of Todd Miller. It disappeared after — well, I turned the house upside down. I haven't painted since."

"Do you think Nora took it?"

He had no idea, and in any case, he would never have confronted her, he said. He had a lot to answer for as it was.

The world was a horrible place, I thought. Yet I felt sure I'd made his suffering worse.

"Alastair," I said to him. "I distracted you that day."

"No. You had nothing to do with this."

"I did. I got you talking about — "

"I left the house angry at Nora. Fucking pissed off at her."

Then I remembered. "You didn't want her having another child."

"I didn't want her having Lyle Miller's child."

"Oh Jesus," I whispered.

Alastair put his arms around me.

"I didn't know. Oh Jesus."

"It's not your fault. It's all right," he said.

"I didn't know."

Grace being an only child, I'd gotten him upset, blurting it out, making the new baby real to him so that he hit the gas and killed Todd Miller and I wept as he held me, stroking my hair, my cheek, drying my tears until I was tingling inside, salty and wet as a breaker's slap, and he drew me down to the ground.

Day vanished, time spun through the hours, the shadows grew, the long silences between our words spreading out beach-like to the edge of the sound, and the silence itself had a texture of infinite softness, a thing made of sand. I could feel its coolness on my toes, damp as the tide going out with the low shush of its breath, a thing of unspeakable beauty, a deep consolation to the soul.

"Just touch me," I said. "That's all."

Be careful, I can hurt you, said his touch and I felt something turn inside him, earth moving from day to night. For a moment I felt afraid of a stranger, a rough man much larger than I was, more in need, but I came at his touch, and so did he, and I held him, and that was enough. Afterwards he took my hand and kissed it and I felt his cheek, wet against my skin.

"It was never your fault," he whispered.

After a while, he said he had something to give me. From his shirt pocket he pulled out an object, then told me to open my hand. On it he placed Alison's gold ring.

"Saw you that day through the window," he said.

"You took it?"

"I asked," he replied. "My mother wanted me to have it."

"You should keep it then," I said.

"No." He took me in his arms, put his lips on mine again. I

felt his tongue inside my mouth, the beating of his heart, the sorrow of his gentle drawing back. He held me and he stroked and kissed my hair. "I just want you to know that it was not your fault," he said. "So that you can get on with your life."

I told him that he was the kindest man I had ever met.

"Claire, you're leaving home. One day you'll get over all of this."

Meaning him.

"Never," I said.

"Life's for getting over."

"You think so?"

"Why we're here," he said. "Whole damn reason."

"I'll prove you wrong," I whispered.

* * *

Once or twice more we met in those early mornings on the beach. We found sheltered corners, we talked and embraced, and before I left for college, he gave me the pine cone he'd found in the northern woods of his childhood.

"You don't want to keep it?" I asked.

"It's the past," he said. "Will you hold it for me?"

I told him yes, not realizing what he meant.

How relieved he looked. He held me in his arms and stroked my hair. "Thank you for everything," he whispered. "I hope there are no hard feelings."

I pulled away and looked at him. "Over what?"

"Over what — we did."

I laughed at his shyness. We hadn't even gone all the way, I reminded him. What a quaint phrase, *all the way*, an odd admission of what we might have done, one from which we would both draw very different conclusions.

"It was lovely," I said.

"I'll miss you when you go."

"I'll give you my address."

I wrote it down for him. He folded the paper and placed it in his shirt pocket, over his heart.

* * *

It would be years before I understood how injured Alastair was. As time passed, he made me think of that radio I'd once broken open, a transmitter of warnings I didn't want to hear.

18

I WAS AT BOSTON U. when the times were on fire. As a journalism major, I filed stories for the *BU News*. There I met a guy from Linden, an editor and activist named Ron. The previous summer he'd covered the March on Washington and Martin Luther King's brilliant speech. Energized by his passion, I was amazed and delighted to discover a kindred spirit from my own hometown. I was immersed in my new life, hanging out in Harvard Square, catching sets by Dylan and Baez, engaging in intense conversations about civil rights and existentialist philosophy with classmates and newspaper staffers. For a smart kid from the 'burbs, this was the American *rive gauche* — brain-buzz minus absinthe and pack-a-day Gauloises. This was how I'd longed to live.

Then I heard from Alastair. *Would it be possible to come visit you?* he wrote.

I didn't want to see him.

It seemed long ago, like summer, like its faded swimsuits and dresses, their pale colours melancholy in the brilliance of autumn; how you want to fold them up and put them away so that you will not find yourself stranded in a vanished season, grieved by the passing of time.

I couldn't bring myself to say no.

I told him he could come, but that I also had a story to file and a paper due.

On Columbus Day weekend, Alastair came to Boston, and we walked through the city's elegant gardens, their gold and flame and russet leaves. He shuffled along in workingman's clothes, boots and flannels and loose-fitting pants. How awkward I felt. He was almost as old as my dad. Yet over lunch he was inquisitive, interested in hearing about my studies and my campus life, and I found myself starting to relax. It felt as if Alastair had shifted roles, becoming a kindly uncle passing through town, one who promises your parents he'll take you out for a decent dinner of non-campus food. Casting him as a relative likely to report back to my folks, I decided to sparkle, to make a great impression. I told him about my two As in Poli Sci and French, my first big assignment for the BU *News*, and how cool it was to cross the bridge into Cambridge and hang out in Harvard Square. I didn't mention Ron. In turn, Alastair told me how happy he was that I was enjoying college, how glad he felt that he, too, had good news to share. He'd be allowed a visit with Grace at Thanksgiving, he said, and he smiled his handsome, thoughtful, serious smile. *What a dear old friend*, I thought. Yet I sensed that I was kidding myself, deliberate in my efforts to erase the encounter that had given Alastair hope enough to visit me. He'd become far more than just a neighbour, an avuncular presence in my new life. He was looking at me as a man looks at a woman. I tried to ignore it.

Alastair suggested a walk in the Common after lunch. There he found a park bench, sat me down and took my hand in his.

"You made me very happy," he said. "I want you to know that."

"Thank you."

"I mean last summer."

"It was nothing."

He gripped my hands, his eyes meeting mine. "You gave me

my life back. Do you remember how I said 'life's for getting over?'"

I did remember. Yes.

"You told me you would prove me wrong."

"Did I?"

"Just by your kindness. Your trust in me. Your letting me —" He hesitated. "I love you, Claire."

I didn't answer.

"Go live your life, finish college, and —" He paused. "If life means us to be together, I'll be here if you'd like to marry me."

I was stunned.

"It wasn't like that for me," I began. Floundering in a swamp of thoughts, I felt stuck. I couldn't hurt Alastair. I couldn't lie to him, either.

"I just wanted — to know what it was like," I said at last. "That's all."

I couldn't look at him. When at last I did, I saw that his eyes were full of grief.

You are my very life, said his gaze, and in it I could feel the weight of all he had suffered, grief I had no mind or heart to bear. Then he took my hand and pressed his lips to the ring I was wearing still. I glanced around, hoping that none of my college friends were traipsing through the Common, glancing my way and wondering what I was up to with this rough-looking man.

"Sometimes things happen for a reason," he said.

"I'm too young for you," I replied.

He sighed, and was quiet for a moment. Then he kissed my forehead. "Your life's ahead, Claire. God bless."

I looked at my watch, told him I had a meeting, told him I was running late.

I ran off.

19

IN THE NEW YEAR, Ron Miller and I began dating. As *BU News* staffers, we covered the civil rights rallies at Boston U. and Harvard. "My Uncle Lyle says the likes of us should be shot," he'd remark as he clicked photos of demonstrators with placards. In between assignments, we'd talk about home. Ron knew about Lyle and Nora and Grace; he'd also heard about Alastair and the accident. He kept his distance from his uncle and his second wife, as his own parents did. He couldn't stand Linden. He never wanted to go back.

Two years passed. In the time of Vietnam, we fell in love and Ron asked me to marry him. He graduated and when he received his draft notice, we decided to leave for Canada. Concerned as my parents were about their neighbours' reactions, we did not return to Linden. We held our wedding at Boston U.'s college chapel.

Days before our marriage, I received a letter, the envelope written in a woman's careful script, the letter itself in a shaky, unfamiliar hand.

June 4th, 1966

Dear Claire,
    I understand you may be moving to Canada. Grace is in Toronto, which is why I am writing. I will give

you her latest address. If you go north, will you find
her and give her my love? Will you look out for her?
I think of you often, for your kindness touched my
heart.
I will always remember you.
Fondly, Alastair.

The letter stunned me. I felt that I hadn't given him anything.
The second page of his note was written by his mother who,
from the looks of things, had also addressed the envelope.

Alastair has had several bouts of depression, and he
cannot travel, but he wanted to write to you. Grace
has gone to Toronto and will attend art school in the
fall. I will pay for her education, but it would ease
her dad's anxiety to know that you might locate and
befriend his daughter who writes, but keeps changing
addresses. Claire, you remember that a few years ago,
I asked you if you would be a friend to Grace. I ask
you this again to console and reassure my son who is
deeply distressed. He trusts you more than anyone. He
believes you can save her.

I wonder what Alison knew about us.
I would write and tell her yes.
Poor Alastair. The irony wasn't lost on me, that I was off to
spend the rest of my life in his native land. On my way into
exile, I felt chastened, realizing what a troubled man he was,
fearing that I'd made his condition worse. It would be years
before I understood that a grown man should never have
approached a naïve teenager, that his suffering did not begin
with me.

Yet I know that my first sexual longing was my own, and

my soul still insists on the mystery of the body, the wound of loneliness for which sex is solace and a blessing.

For a moment, I did love Alastair.

Nothing is simple, nothing at all.

* * *

June 5th, 1966

Dear Alastair,

Thank you for your kind words. I have been very negligent and I am sorry that I have not written to you. Yes it is true, I am planning to move. I will live in Toronto and I will finish college there.

Please tell your mother that I will do my best to locate Grace, and I promise that I will look out for her as best I can. You can count on me to do that.

I paused, my pen hovering over the page.

Ron Miller and I are getting married, and heading north together. I look forward to life in your beautiful country.

I paused again, then wrote.

Stay well.

* * *

Ron and I married and raised two children in a charming old brick-and-gabled house in east-end Toronto. He practiced law, I became a journalist, and life's been good to us in our adopted country. Yet even with my friends and my profession, I have spent these years as a wanderer through a northern silence I will never understand, a haunted place where in everyday speech I can hear the wind that howls across the prairie between each human being and her neighbour. Nothing stands before the wind, and no voice abides in this country's open space. Canada was to be my exile, my life's work, my struggle through Grace's suffering to see who Alastair was.

Grace

20

YELLOW SATURATES EVERYTHING. It's the only colour Grace sees, a revolt of the delicate receptors of the eye, a pressure on the optic nerve, or so she thinks — a condition she can only relieve by painting. Real paint, not some little paint-roller icon you click on the computer: rag-less, mess-less, lifeless. *Hell, no.* She's on a mission — she and her band of street artists — a wild phoenix rising from the dull ash of everyday Toronto, out to paint whole buildings bright as egg yolks, highways and bridges in a scorch of fire-orange. As it was in the beginning of this optical storm that has seized her over the past year with its dazzling monochromes of emerald, indigo, crimson.

Grace won't see a specialist for her eyes. She's sure they'll pigeonhole her condition (*condition!*) with a goddamn name, *chronic idiopathic chromatosis*, meaning they don't know what the fuck's going on with all those colours, and once you've turned fifty, they could care less. Well she cares, because she knows what's going on. She dropped too much acid when she was a kid. All those bad trips and now she's collecting air miles, that's the truth.

Look on the bright side. Built-in art. Never have to wait for inspiration.

She thinks she's blessed.

Grace's gone to work on behalf of buggered-up people like herself, helping them paint the city aflame, scrounging leftover paints, brushes, rollers from artsy friends who aren't keen on breaking the law but who love her idea, its edge of defiance. In this tough new century, it's a hell of a lot less depressing, they'd say, than giving a loonie to some poor soul begging for change. They all know Gracie Luce, installation artist and part-time anarchist who teaches homeless youth to provoke the hell out of wired and well-to-do Toronto. Her rich patrons love her. Most of all, love watching her.

Love her because the squeegee kids are fighting back, rogue painters by night at the Bloor Viaduct, on the buildings in the CNE grounds in the city's west end, in subway tunnels and in shabby laneways where street people huddle against the cold. She's turning the streets into a peoples' school of art, drenching whole city blocks in vibrant monochrome dressed with lavish ribbons of graffiti. It looks like a homeless confectioner's deranged idea, a pastry-shop of a skyline. She thinks of Marie Antoinette, of her fondness for sweets.

So do the critics. *Let 'em eat you-know-what,* says the *Star. Cakes 'R Us.*

An artist's insurrection, that's what those in the know are calling it: *the writing's on the wall, City Hall,* said the NOW front page. Literal truth, but Grace doesn't own a computer so she can't check out blogs or newspaper websites. During her colour-storms, her eyes can't see to read. She's a binge-painter. She has no conceptual scheme, she's following her body's urge to spread an infection of colour. She spends her days gathering blankets, sandwiches, hot cocoa for the street kids, whatever gives them strength to work. Sometimes she sleeps alongside them, encamped in the underpass adjoining the ravine.

They're starting to get cheeky, thank God, she thinks. They hand out flyers with their squeegee jobs. *Home(less) improvements! Help spruce up those underpasses! Help give those gratings a new coat of paint! Give!*

The city brightens as derelict buildings and busy tunnels shout in red and yellow, violet, and green. No arrests are made — who'd dare? Not when *The New York Times* does a travel spread naming Toronto the funkiest city on the continent, not when U.S. tourists are lining up to book rooms. Knowing that she can't always get to a computer, her dad mails her the *Times* article — her old man who's getting on in years, the last person she wants worried about her health. She asks her friend Claire to read her the piece, explaining that she couldn't see the tiny *Times* print, that the lineup for the library computer would have wasted her afternoon.

Claire's in a hurry. She and Ron have to catch a plane. They're off to his Uncle Lyle's funeral in New York.

Grace hasn't spoken to her stepdad in years, so she's not going. Ron hates Lyle, too. He and Claire were headed for a family reunion when the guy kicked off. Grace figured Lyle timed his exit with his usual fascist precision, knowing it was the only way he'd get any mourners. "You're too cynical," said Claire, but then she giggled. Soft as butter on a hot day, good old Claire.

She reads Grace the *Times* article. "The city should be proud of you," she says.

Grace shrugs. She's minding their house for a couple of days, and once she's alone, she helps herself to a cold beer. Then she roots around in the large pine sideboard, finds the opener and notices in the cluttered drawer a tiny demitasse spoon. Its tarnished silver looks ignored. She pockets it and drinks down her beer.

Claire's a reporter, and she doesn't notice.

Or maybe she does.

A stem vase, a mirror, a tiny clay doll. A house jammed with *stuff*. Half-hidden by a huge potted fern in a corner of the living room is an ancient family photo, very formal, one that from the looks of things had been taken when Claire was in college. It was faded, one of those dust-collectors that nobody's looked at for years. Only her eye catches something, a tiny photo stuck in a corner of the frame. *Who the hell's the gal,* she wonders. *Looks like Claire around the eyes.* Her and a handsome guy. She pulls it out, turns it over. *Betty-Ann and Don at his senior prom,* it says. *New York, 1962. Christ, Claire's sister. Used to look after me, used to call me an ugly potato. What the hell does she want with this?* She remembers Don Wheeler, the mayor's kid. *An aid worker in El Salvador,* her father had told her with sorrow in his voice. *A death squad found him.* She gazes at the photo of the woman and the lost man. Then she slips it into her pocket. She can use Don's picture in a collage. Betty-Ann she'll slice out. At home she's got an Exacto blade.

Most of the time, she doesn't know why she steals. She makes up excuses. It's clutter-reduction, not theft. Skim off the surplus, smash up the cheap junk, recycle it all as found art. Claire and Ron don't care, don't notice, just keep adding more.

After she's finished her beer, she calls her dad to thank him for the *Times* spread.

"Are you coming down?" he asks her.

"For what?"

"The funeral."

Earlier he'd called to ask her that. She'd said she'd come, meaning sometime, for a visit. "Maybe," she answers, but only because her dad would like to see her. "I'm getting ready."

"To come?"

"To start a new project."

"Thought you just did."

"The Royal Bank could use a coat of paint," she tells him.

Grace can hear a silence full of questions. *Are you sure that's legal, Gracie? You could end up in jail.*

"I hope you've got permission," he says.

Grace laughs.

She hears a pause at his end. "Come down, honey."

"Maybe."

"You might want to see your mother." His voice is sad.

Grace lights a cigarette. "She can come and help me paint."

"She's sick. Bad heart."

"I'm sorry," says Grace.

"Lyle's illness hit her real hard."

You should feel for her, dad?

"She's your mother. Maybe you want to see her, is all."

Grace doesn't. She says goodbye. He wants so much to be her father, and she understands that. He'd made a modest success of his life, retiring on the proceeds of his house-painting business. It was small, only four trucks, and he would have turned it over to her but she felt overwhelmed by the idea. *Don't be, hon*, her dad said. *You never know till you try.* His words were hacked out of the hard clay of suffering, words that said *I hold you dear.* She couldn't bring herself to try.

"They put an electrical current through his brain," said her mom when Grace was twelve. "He may forget you." She'd wept with rage, that she'd be snatched from his memory like this.

Her father no longer painted.

"Illness runs in families," said her mother.

* * *

Grace loves her father and yet there are times when she feels possessed by him, by the wordless and driven part of him that needed the language of colour. She feels him inside her when her fingers smoulder like cigarettes, remembering how as a kid she imagined electroshock as punishment, electrocution, her father's body tangled in an angry noose of smoke and leather straps. Now when she feels afraid, she thinks of this, as if she must paint to compensate for what he lost, giving it form before his torturers catch up with her.

Meanwhile Gracie's Guerrillas are chitchat under the gabled roofs of chic downtown. "Canadian Living: The Homeless Installation" reads the Arts headline in *The Globe and Mail.* Claire left it for her on the coffee table, but it's one thing she won't steal. She's been asked to comment, to give interviews, to join her colleagues in the warm indoors of Toronto's art scene. She always declines.

I can't, I can't.

It's not all art she's brought to birth. This broken dam of her mind, this deluge of colour's a driven thing, an instinct for dissipation, what cold weather does to leaves. *They unstick from the branch, right? First they're stuck, then they unstick from what the hell's that thing called?* She strains to remember. *Abscission layer, that's it. I saw it on TV.*

God takes care of the leaves, then brings them down.

Oh God, for a hurricane, a wind. One night she woke up freezing in the laneway. She knows enough to be afraid of this.

Grace stares at her pale face in the mirror, her thick black hair streaked with grey, swept up on her head in a swirl of tortoise-shell combs. She dresses in woollen wraps from Peru, Indian cottons and lace-up boots, stuff she buys second-hand on Bathurst and Queen. Yet she assembles it all with style (so she's been told), dressing to reveal the anarchy of her mind, as well as her prodigious talent. Her found art hangs in galleries, her work's collected, she's won prizes. She saved enough to buy a small loft near Parliament Street — her only wealth, all she owns. Her money never lasts.

She hates indoors.

She'd like to see her dad, but she's fearful of planes and even more afraid of returning to Linden, to a place of so much sorrow. Her dad understood this, and he'd come to visit her from time to time. Her mother's as distant as a sunset, a woman she no longer knows. When Nora and Lyle sent her away to boarding school, she'd accepted the fact that they'd never again be part of her life. It was nothing she could put into words. She'd caused this to happen; she was a dead branch that had to be pruned for the health of the tree. On the make at fifteen, she'd been scared of the rough guys she'd looked for and enjoyed. "You'll end up like your dad," said Nora, and Grace thought of her father wired up and convulsing. Afraid, she tried to study, but she wasn't allowed to draw, and her fingers burned, as if lit from inside. She fled to Toronto and got herself roughed up again. Returning to school was anguish and the memory of it rumbles underfoot, troubles the earth so that she feels the tremor, the cracks in her soul, too parched for tears. There's no home, no place of birth to which she can return. Yet she still has her father.

I'm alive. Like it or not.

She gets up, paces the floor, walks from room to room in Claire and Ron's skinny little east-end townhouse. She pockets a linen napkin and a jar of marmalade. In the bedroom, she heads for the bureau. It's a mindless thing, a habit of hers to pick through the contents of Claire's jewellery boxes. There's a glut of forgotten baubles her friend no longer wears, an untidy tangle of earrings, pendants, glass and ceramic beads. She's calmed by the silken feel of tumbled stones. Now and again, she'll help herself to some.

Her favourite discard is a plain gold ring. Inside it are the initials *A. & T. L.* Claire said it was a gift from Grandmother Lange whose poetry she'd admired, who hoped she'd research their family roots in northern Ontario. In her hand she feels her father's past, the evidence he's lost of it. He must have a birthday coming up, her dad. *Neat idea.* She tucks the ring into her backpack, locks up the house and heads downtown to paint.

21

THEY HAD A LITTLE HISTORY, herself and Claire.
"I promised your grandmother," said Claire when she found her in Toronto. That was back in the sixties.

"Fucking what did you promise?"

"That I'd be your friend."

My guide dog. Daddy's little pet chihuahua.

Except that if the promise were true, Claire might have come north with a wad of Granny's dough. It wouldn't hurt to be nice. Granny was paying for art school and Grace had told her she'd help with a waitressing job, but it wasn't working out. She'd been in Toronto since April. She'd made enough money to drop some acid, and then she got herself fired for being too tripped out to show up for work. If she had any smarts at all, she'd stay calm and listen.

It turned out that Claire had been in T.O. only a few weeks, and that she'd heard from Granny Alison that Grace had gone north. Claire had known to find her with all the runaways and artsy types in Yorkville, strung out like laundry on a clothesline, a kid with a space-for-rent look in her eyes, sitting on someone's front stairs smoking. Whip-thin, dark glasses, long black hair, a flower embroidered on her jeans. Grace told her she was living with three bikers, rent-free. *Their gal,* she smirked. *And she's dumb enough to believe it,* Grace thought. *Check out the dropped jaw.*

"That'll look good on your résumé," said Claire.

"It's work," Grace replied.

"Smartass."

"Yeah, so?"

"So how do you think your dad would feel if he knew?"

"Knew what?"

"How you were living," said Claire. "In a dump with — "

"He won't," said Grace.

"He'll ask. He's your dad."

"I'm lucky if he knows my name."

"Huh?"

Grace shrugged. "Shock'll do that. He just about lives on a mental ward."

It wasn't true, but it made Claire wilt like a dead flower. Grace smiled. She threw her cigarette butt on the ground and stomped it out.

"So what was that promise?" she asked her.

"That we'd be friends. But first —"

There's always a catch, Grace thought.

"Quit handing me a load of crap. Tell me what's up with your dad."

"Why, so you can fuck him again?"

"Watch your mouth, Gracie. That's a lie."

Grace stared at the ground. "Dad's not well," she said.

"But he knows who you are."

"And he knows who *you* are."

She watched the words work in Claire like rat poison on a greedy, cheese-loving rodent. Slow-motion collapse, her guts caving in.

Not quite.

Claire sighed. "You could use a new life," she said.

Grace looked at her watch. "Suppertime," she said. "Time to sweeten up the boys."

"Oh for Chrissakes, drop that bullshit."

"And do what?"

She felt Claire's stare at her wasted frame. "When did you eat last?" she asked.

* * *

Grace went home with her.

"Dad could have sent me to art school," she said over dinner. "But he got sick again." She dug into her food with care, as if some further explanation were buried under the mashed potatoes.

"Are you going to classes?" asked Claire.

"School doesn't start 'till September."

"And you have money?"

Grace didn't look up. "The guys treat me good," she murmured.

Claire invited her to stay with them for a while.

Grace paused. "I've got obligations."

"Such as?"

"Cleaning. Groceries." *Since that's what they pay me for,* Grace thought.

Claire told her she'd help her out with funds.

Grace lowered her eyes again.

"You'll stay a while? Is that a yes?"

"I'll tell my buddies I've found other work."

She stayed overnight. In her room, she looked in the mirror and saw her mother's conniving look. Later she overheard her hosts.

"You don't believe that guff, do you?" Ron asked.

"Grace's had a hard life," said Claire.

"Yeah, well, it's made her a hard little bitch."

"You don't understand. Her grandmother asked me to look after her."

So lick my boots, Grace thought.

She couldn't stop that cruel lash of insult in her head. Meanness wrapped itself around her tongue like the soft, moist inside of a chocolate. *So I'm a shit.* It was instinctive, satisfying, the wish of her own bricked-up soul to break Claire open, make her admit that she'd messed around with her dad. She'd never forgotten the look on his face after he came back from Boston, his soul flayed, his eyes driven wild. There were savage ways to make somebody look like that.

Only she had no proof that anything much had happened with him and Claire. Just the knowledge that she and her father had been beaten by the same club, and that was Nora. Now he looked beaten again.

* * *

She and Claire had been friends once, sort of. Not since Todd died, though — not really. Claire had been in the truck that day, distracting her dad. Good, sweet Claire, taking his mind off the road.

In her hands she could feel her mother's rage, as if she were possessed.

She returned to her flat and started art school. The bikers moved on and some classmates joined her. In her studio, Grace worked hard at huge and violent canvases, paint bleeding from old wounds, colours electric with outrage. After a while, she stopped feeling devoured by hatred. If she could paint all the time, she thought, she would not want revenge. It was as a child that she first imagined painting an entire city until it burned with colour and consumed her in the flames.

Claire stayed in touch with her. If Ron were working late, she'd invite her for dinner. Often they'd talk about art and books and music, but sometimes Grace would nudge at Claire's sore spot, bobbing for it like a Halloween apple, veering toward the subject of her father. Grace couldn't explain her own appetite for provocation, an enticement to stray into danger zones, a drive to see Claire erupt in rage, screaming at her that she was obsessed with sex.

Only needling didn't work. Claire was too clever, too calm. *Your dad gave you artistic talent,* she'd say, *and he gave me friendship.* That was all.

One evening, Claire looked confident and full of joy.

"We're going to have a baby," she said.

For a minute, Grace said nothing. "I should, too," she said at last. "I'd get a baby bonus then."

"It wouldn't keep you in crayons."

Grace shrugged. "Pays better than fucking for a living."

Claire didn't even looked shocked. She laughed. "Come on, Gracie."

"Come on, what?"

"Be happy with me!"

Something stabbed at Grace, a wordless anguish sheathed in rage that Claire was so self-possessed, so immune to the poison that had formed and nourished her. She could not bear feeling so loveless.

At last she acknowledged that the pregnancy was good news.

"Are you quitting your job?" she asked.

"At the *Star?*" Claire seemed puzzled by the question. "They'll give me maternity leave."

Grace heard the kettle whistling in the kitchen. "I'll make tea," she said.

Claire looked wary, and Grace knew why. Claire was a health-food nut, and the *Star* had run a front-page story about a girl from the art college with an unwanted pregnancy who'd bled to death from overdosing on tansy tea. *Maybe she's got tansy in the cupboard,* Grace thought. *Doesn't want me near the stuff.*

"I'll take care of it," said Claire. She went into the kitchen, then came back with a pot of mint tea. She looked Grace in the eye. "You're an open book," she said.

"Oh?"

"The only one you scare is yourself."

"Just so you know, I don't screw for money."

"Just so you know, my herbal teas are harmless. I know the reporter who wrote that story in the *Star*. About the pregnant kid who died."

"Stuff works."

Claire frowned.

"Homegrown tansy's like Russian roulette. Depends on the dose."

"What are you saying?"

"I always keep a stash on hand." Grace stood up and rummaged in her pockets, as if she were looking for some. "Try a pinch in your Mom-Mix," she said. "Cheap thrills."

Claire strode over to her and pointed to the door. "Get out of here," she said.

Grace didn't move.

"Are you deaf?"

Grace's body waited for a rain of slaps.

Claire pointed to the door. "Out," she said, as if for a dog. "Out," she repeated. She held the door wide open.

Grace left.

* * *

Grace wrote Claire an apology. *I don't know why I did that. I just know that you bring out the worst in me. In fairness to you, I'll stick to painting.* She wished Claire and her family a good life.

Avoiding her old friend, Grace worked hard, graduated from art college and made a name for herself. Art worked like a serum that eased the venom out of her, but at other times she felt possessed by her mother's cruelty, certain she could never exorcise it, wondering if this battle fuelled her art, afraid to relinquish the ghosts that tormented her.

Claire didn't try to contact her, except to inform her when her kids were born. The birth announcements made Grace want to see her old friend, yet she felt unworthy of Claire's friendship. She hated her, she loved her. She painted in a fury, finding herself on the edge of one precarious relationship after another. For a while, obsessed by that lost friendship, she'd bring home rough men and a few unwary, passive women until, realizing that nothing could assuage her sense of loss, she chose to remain alone.

Fifteen years passed, and Grace's grandmother Alison died. Her dad called and invited her to the funeral, but she couldn't bring herself to go. At the thought of facing her father's grief as well as her own, she wept. *Don't cry, Gracie*, he said to her. *She had a peaceful end.* But crying opened a sluice of grief, a place in her heart long shut, and those words of her father's made her imagine he was talking about her, an utter failure (despite her success) who'd only find comfort in life's end. She wept because she felt desolate about her life, and her dad, even far away, was at least a comfort. He told her she should try to get some help, to sort out her feelings. *I'd end up getting shocked, like you*, she thought. *I'd never paint again.*

Later she considered going to the funeral, but she felt as if she'd be a distraction and a burden to her father at a difficult time. Instead she painted a condolence card for him, a vivid likeness of Alison copied from a photo Grace took long ago. Her dad called to thank her. *What a gift you have, Gracie. You've made her live*, he said. She felt better then.

Grace herself received a note of sympathy from Claire, who asked if they could meet at her office. Curious, Grace agreed. After all this time, she felt anxious enough to show up in her best suit of clothes — a denim jacket and crisp, new jeans. In the waiting area, she could hear Claire coming before she saw her, the gun-burst staccato of her heels on polished floors. Claire looked the same as she'd remembered her, slim and composed, trim jacket, skirt and heels. *Probably gets a colour job on her hair by now.* She welcomed Grace into her office. Apart from condolences, there were no preliminaries. Grace didn't expect any.

"Before she died," said Claire, "Your grandmother asked me to administer a trust fund."

"She made you rich."

"It's for you, Grace."

The weary look on Claire's face took her aback. "You're doing this for me?" she asked.

"Your grandmother was very kind to me. I wouldn't say no."

Grace didn't want the money. She told Claire she didn't feel she deserved it.

"Someday you might need it," said Claire.

"I'll be dead by then."

Claire looked concerned. "You've done well, Grace. Your grandmother would be proud."

"Only I'm not much good with money."

"I'll be looking after it," said Claire. "You don't have to worry."

It surprised Grace, how those words touched her.

"What can I do for you?" she asked.

That impulse to kindness surprised Grace even more. She prayed that whatever Claire asked her to do, it wouldn't provoke anger, wouldn't expose some long-forgotten bitterness. There was no reason to resent Claire. It had been years since that business with her dad, and he'd survived. He'd made the best of things, even if he no longer painted.

Claire had something in mind. She asked Grace if she might

house-sit from time to time while she and Ron took the occasional weekend off, and Grace agreed.

Then she mentioned something else to her, a clutch of paintings in Alison's effects. She'd told Claire that these belonged to Grace, and that long ago, she'd put them into storage, keeping them safe for the day when her peripatetic grandchild would settle down. About to be sent to boarding school, Grace remembered begging her grandmother to store them, bundling them up herself, concealing their imagery from the woman's eyes. Her grandmother had laughed and said, *nothing shocks me, dear*, but she'd raised no objections.

The storage people had already packed and shipped them, said Claire, and all Grace had to do was clear them through customs when they arrived. Grace smiled. These were small treasures she wanted back, ticking clocks wired to hidden fuses. She herself would be their match, struck and lit.

It was after this exchange that Grace began house-sitting on long weekends for Claire and Ron. She felt overwhelmed by their home, a brick-and-gabled townhouse, a chi-chi reno in the east end. More than that, she felt wrapped inside its sensuous embrace of textures and fabrics, colours and perfumes. It was then that she began pocketing small things: an old wristwatch, a jazz CD, a floral teacup, a fountain pen. *They've got two computers. What's she need a pen for?* Theft came to her with so much ease that she never thought to call it what it was. She swiped a pine cone, so damn brittle it fell apart in her pocket. She threw it out. She kept stealing, but she'd forgotten, if she ever knew, what it was she'd wanted here. It was nothing she could find or name.

22

IT'S FOUR A.M., ANOTHER NIGHT of painting done. Wrapped in memories, Grace comes inside.

Today's the day they hold a wake for Vile Lyle, she thought. *If I were there, I'd spit on his coffin.*

After she'd locked up Claire's house, she met her reno-team and they went to work. They finished painting a church sky-blue so that people would try to walk through it and crash into hard reality. Some minister liked the idea and let them do it. *Christ, what day is this? Sunday? God'll notice. God's colour, made of light.* God hurts her eyes. Gripping the banister, Grace hauls herself upstairs. There's nothing medically wrong with her. *Paint without ceasing.*

Claire's on her side. Apart from her grandmother's trust fund, her old neighbour still puts money into her work, but not into her pocket. Instead Claire supports the Canadian Street-Art Foundation, where she sits on the board of directors. She looks enough like Grace to be her sister, apart from the fact that she's stylish in jeans and a soft leather jacket, her hair blunt-cut. Grace prefers lace-up leather boots, denim cutoffs, and beaded Indian cotton. A sixties throwback, she nonetheless prides herself on her turn-of-the-twentieth-century edge, red flames tattooed on her arms. She knows she probably looks deranged. She knows she'll never be Claire's equal.

Yet over time, Grace notices that her feelings have changed

toward her old friend. Without thinking herself unworthy, she now admires her. It's a kind of crush she has, like a teenage kid with a teacher. Claire has a quickness to her, a wary manner, yet her eyes defeat this with their clear-water depth, and seeing this, Grace is sometimes overwhelmed with longing. Yet Claire's beyond her, purposeful, made from finer clay. Grace knows she loves Claire as a flea loves a cat. Her love spoils. Her life will not be long.

* * *

Two days pass and Claire's back from the funeral, slugging away at the *Star*. She calls to tell Grace that she's doing a write-up on the homeless art phenomenon, as she calls it. *It's going to be posted on the website, along with a YouTube video. It'll go viral.* Grace listens.

"Would you let me quote you?" Claire asks.

"What for?"

Laughter. "You started this."

"Didn't," says Grace. "God did."

"God doesn't give interviews. Come on, Gracie. You're famous."

"No."

"Yes. It's time to be a little more outgoing."

Grace paused. "Only if you let me check my email."

"Huh?"

"Aren't you bringing your laptop?"

Claire laughed.

All past resentments aside, Grace understands that she owes Claire more than she can repay. She tells her she'll talk to her, and she invites her to her loft. Even so, she wonders why Claire would bother. To her mind, the multicoloured city is eloquence enough. Claire tells her that a *Star* videographer is shooting everything, uploading it onto the Internet:

daisy-yellow heating grates, rose-and-violet bridges, the Bloor Viaduct (once known for suicides), now a calming sea-blue-green, a haven for the troubled. The street artists are keen to talk to the world.

"Home decor for the homeless," says Grace. She talks about the fun of painting underpasses with a gang of kids. Claire clicks away on her laptop.

"What keeps you going?" she asks.

"Fire," says Grace. "The Demon Colour, burning me up."

"Say what you said on the phone," Claire urges.

"What, about property values going up? On cardboard boxes?"

"Uh-huh." Claire's eyes are on the screen.

Grace smiles to herself. "Art's just the start," she says.

"Of what?" asks Claire.

"Of warfare. Aerial bombardment of the Royal Bank Tower. A job for the Homeless Air Force. You could build cheap housing on that space."

"Smartass." Claire snaps her laptop shut.

"Done so soon?"

"I've got enough."

"Can I check my email now?"

Claire shoves the laptop toward Grace, who goes online.

It works every time, Grace thinks. Her interviews come to a quick end as soon as she tries out any subversion stronger than paint, any challenge to authority (this is Canada, after all), any goddamned *humour*, for chrissakes. Her anarchist views are never quoted, never seen as such. Instead there's a summary line or two in the papers, *as verbally incoherent as she's visually brilliant* or in a critical journal, *profound disturbance is evident in her thoughts, no doubt the wellspring of her innovative art.*

What crap.

She glances at the screen, at an unopened email. The subject line reads *your mother*. She clicks on it.

Shit, who sent that? My fucking semi-brother, John.

What the hell, don't you answer your phone? it said. *Mom had a massive heart attack. She's in North Linden Hospital. Get your fucking ass down here, if you're sober enough to read this.*

Grace hits Delete.

*　*　*

"Is there something wrong?" asked Claire.

"My ex-mother had a heart attack."

"I'm sorry."

"I'm not. Nora can go croak without me."

In the depth of Claire's gaze, there's sorrow and bewilderment. Grace feels this shift in her mood, as you do with the air when the wind comes up before rain.

"I didn't mean to put you off," says Grace.

"You make me think of your dad," Claire answers.

"How come my dad?"

"You get straight to the point."

"My dad before he got sick. Yeah."

Dig in, Gracie. Every chance you get. Pain's zipping across Claire's face like a jaywalker on a busy street. Grace feels seized by some monstrous thing — it was that email that did it, Nora's spirit slipping its filthy hands into her body, turning up the gauge as she grips Claire's slender arm and leads her over to the cupboard on the far wall.

As Grace approaches, she can hear it, *tick-tock, tick-tock*, feeling the grit of a struck match, a fuse about to be lit. *Thanks, Grandma, for holding on to these.* She opens the cupboard door and pulls out a canvas. In Claire's eyes she sees a flicker of awe, as if they were reflecting light, the beauty of her father's

112

finest work. It's a small painting, his study of affronted innocence, the child's eyes dark with premonition, his hair so gold that her eyes can feel the brightness.

"He was my pal," she says to Claire. "He sat so still for this."

For a moment, Claire says nothing.

"How beautiful," she whispers.

"Did my old man tell you it was gone?"

Claire nodded. "He was upset that he'd lost it."

"I hid it under the mattress. Dad wanted to take a knife to it."

She remembered how distraught her father was as he tore the house apart. Her poor dad never found the painting, never thought to question her, then became "a danger to himself," as the law says. He ended up in the hospital. Maybe he knew he'd never paint again. Maybe he wouldn't have cracked up if she hadn't hidden his finest work.

Grace knows she should tell Claire the whole story, but something's gone awry, and she can almost taste her suffering, sure she's found the fault-line where this quiet soul will break.

"That was in Granny's stash," says Grace. "The one you had sent."

"He was talented," Claire whispers.

"*Was,* is right," says Grace.

She pulls out the worst of her dad's abstractions, one she dubbed *Melted Ice Cream Variations*. To her mind, it showed what shock treatment did to her father's painting. Also part of the stash, the canvas was awash in birthday-card sentiments, dribbly and pearly-soft, gentle with greys and lavender-pinks, a 1950s idea from the 'burbs of something called Modern Art.

It wasn't his fault the fire had been doused in his heart.

1963, his last attempt, and he'd given it to her. She could cry.

Claire touches it, then steps back. She looks shocked herself.

"Yeah, right," says Grace.

Claire doesn't speak, and the silence unnerves Grace as she

watches her gaze at the painting. Claire reaches out to touch it again and a shy moment passes before she takes her wallet out of her purse, opens it, and pulls out a hundred-dollar bill.

"Will you sell it?" she asks.

Grace's eyes fill with tears. She pushes Claire's hand and the money away, takes her dad's worst painting and presses it into her friend's arms. Claire takes it and puts her wallet back in her purse. They stare at each other, not knowing what to say.

23

A LONE, GRACE WONDERS WHY the hell Claire wanted to buy that hideous painting, her father's disgrace; why she'd offered to pay *a hundred bucks*. She poured herself a drink, musing over her friend and her wad of bills. Claire didn't know she *stole* a hundred bucks once from Lyle's wallet — caught shit for it, too. Right on the buttocks Nora whacked her with a skillet while she'd drifted off, floating up to the ceiling where she watched Nora flail away at a dummy heap of skin and bones.

Yet look at what she'd done to her father, his life ruined over a painting that she'd stolen. The knife story was pure bullshit. She was a liar and a thief on top of it, and all her digs at Claire changed nothing.

She pulls out the demitasse spoon she filched with the jar of marmalade from Claire's. Opening the jar, she dips it in, licking the sweet jam with slow anticipation. She imagines Claire finding her with the pilfered goods, looking disgusted, showing her the door again.

* * *

Only now it's getting late and there's a long night ahead. Grace packs her gear, heading off for a painting job near the base of Parliament Street. Her team's stoking a fire of saturated reds and tangerine, a hearth in the cold. *You'll see how warm it is*, she says to the street kids as they work into the night, but she's been drinking down the memory of how they crushed her father, and how she might have stopped it with a word. *I found your painting, Dad.* How he sat in the hospital ward, subdued and bland as custard. *I'm getting well, honey*, he'd said to her, but his eyes were chastened, as if this were punishment, what you get when life crushes a sturdy heart and grinds it up into gravel.

As for herself, she stole the painting because her old man had killed her best friend and she wanted him back. She wanted to punish her dad, and she did. She'd wanted to rip Todd's life out of time, holding it forever in the moment before his death. What a liar, look how she'd finagled her grandmother into storing her dad's finest work (and his worst), convincing her that the paintings held some shocking invention of her own. She'd landed her dad a kick in the butt, and mistreated Claire as if she'd done the same thing.

It's late and she brings blankets and pillows for the painters, but when she lies down beside them, she's despondent and she can't sleep. Dazed, she gets up and looks outside at the golden blaze they've painted on the walls of their city. It's then that she feels a grateful calm, aware that death is near, stalking her like a predator, the kind who tempts with dangerous sex. She's sure she's going to find danger, to submit to it with pleasure. She drinks too much, she can always find drugs, there are rotten people who'd love to get their hands on her and wouldn't charge a cent. As she waits in the shadows of the underpass, she understands that it's not a hearth she's painted but a rage of colour, a fury that's burning her alive.

* * *

She survives that evening, waking at dawn, exhausted and in pain, remembering nothing of the night before. Thankful she lives a short walk away, she returns home, hearing the phone ring as she stumbles into her apartment.

"This is John," says the voice on the other end.

"Who?"

"Your brother, sort of."

"Oh, right," answers Grace.

"What the hell, get voice-mail, for chrissakes. I've been calling all night."

"I'm not home at night," she says.

"Well get a goddamn cell-phone then. Mom's in the hospital. Her heart."

"I got your email."

"She's not gonna make it."

"Say goodbye for me."

Then all at once she's angry because he doesn't understand why she won't come. John was too young to know about Todd and Alastair, but it's hopeless to tell her version of the story when long ago, Nora and Lyle turned him away from her and her father. Her grief is buried in the bone's marrow, a story too anguished for words. Sounds erupt from the depths of her body, rage battling sorrow, and she's weeping.

There's a pause at the other end of the line.

"Are you smashed?"

She stops crying. "I'm goddamn sober as a judge."

"Mom used to say you were just like your dad."

Asshole. Grace slams the phone down. *A bastard, just like Lyle. Wants you to lick his goddamn boots, the prick.* She puts on a pot of coffee and lights a cigarette. She knows she should shower, get herself cleaned up. She has to consider what she should do, but her thoughts are worms in tilled soil and they wriggle off into the dark. Some plan would grow in that head of hers. After a while, she calls her father, but she doesn't burden him with words. Long ago he'd asked her to forgive

him. Nothing old is left, and there are no more words to say.
He's not going to visit Nora.

"I don't want to, either," Grace tells him. She hears a pause.

"Your mother's going to die."

"I know."

"Try to forgive her," he says.

"I don't know how," she replies. She hears her father taking in his breath, trying not to cry.

"I want my Gracie to live a long time," he says.

"Don't worry."

"Try to forgive her."

As if Alastair Luce were still trying.

She isn't sure how to forgive her mother, or even what forgiveness means. She dries her eyes. She could use some forgiving herself, but she has no idea how to ask it of her poor old man.

"Gracie," says her dad. "Are you still there?"

She takes a deep breath.

"I was out late last night," she says. *Looking for trouble. Trying to decide whether to live or die.*

"Were you painting?"

She hesitates.

She tells him yes.

* * *

It wasn't until she hung up the phone that a thought came like the slow tingle of a numbed foot waking up, as if all these years she'd been sound asleep and having bad dreams that she'd confused with wakefulness. Now for the first time, she had to face the odd sensation of two feet standing, holding her body upright on the earth. She saw it, felt it, could almost taste it: her father needed her. She felt the anguish of what he must be feeling, the shattering memories of youth and hope destroyed; how he couldn't visit Nora without seeing the woman he'd once loved, how he couldn't avoid Nora without the risk of never letting go. Yet he'd made the only smart decision, and anyway, Nora didn't care if he showed up. *You made the right choice, Dad.*

Thoughts weren't enough, she realized. The guy needed solace and maybe even the comfort of her presence. *Try to forgive her*, he'd said.

Impossible.

Her poor dad.

You've never gone home? Claire asked when Lyle Miller died. Her voice had been sad, concerned, not judgmental. *It's not "home,"* Grace answered, and then she paused. *Dad visits from time to time*, she added. Claire dropped the subject, as Grace had intended. Claire realized she was the last person who should prod her about attending to her father's needs, and Grace had meant to keep her at a distance.

Rotten, treating Claire that way. What a stupid waste of time.

Grace didn't know what to do.

Nora was her mother, about to die. *Like hell I'll go and visit that bitch.*

It felt as if Nora owned the town of Linden, and even if she died, she'd poisoned its wells and polluted its air for good. Grace felt ill, the lead weight of her father's pain leaching into her bones. Yet she couldn't go back.

24

IT WAS ALREADY NOON and Grace felt exhausted and ill. She hadn't slept the night before, and she couldn't remember what she'd been drinking or what sort of sky-high stuff she might have ingested. Or maybe it was paint fumes, car exhaust, toxic life in the underpasses catching up with her. She collapsed on the floor, wrapped herself in an old down bedspread and fell asleep. It wasn't a good sleep, not at first. In her dream, Nora reached in and tore out her insides bare-handed, as if she were gutting a chicken. Blinded by pain, Grace fell into a sleep within her sleep. In darkness, the memory of this ravaging ebbed away from her.

When she woke up, she saw drawn curtains parted, daybreak etching a bold strip of light across her body. She wondered how long she'd slept. The clock said seven a.m. She dozed a while longer, then got up, showered and dressed. She didn't feel great, but at least she was alive.

**

It didn't surprise her later when her father called.

Nora passed away, he told her.

Thank God, she thought.

Just to be kind, she thanked him for telling her.

"Honey, I know how you feel," he said. "So if you don't come down, it's okay."

Then she *felt* him. It was like that pins-and-needles moment when the numbness had passed out of her, as if she could sense kindness, an invitation to speak. She'd never said all that much to her father. In her unhappy youth, he'd tried to reach out, but she'd walled up her feelings, hid them in a fort of anger where she'd vanished.

"She made it rough." Grace felt like crying.

"I know, I know. I still love you."

Grace couldn't speak.

"Gracie?"

She dried her eyes. "Are you okay, Dad?"

"I'm okay."

"Don't let this make you sick, huh?"

"Don't worry."

Grace paused. "Some other time I'll come home. Promise."

* * *

Only afterward did she stop to think that she'd promised him a visit yet again. The same words over and over, clumps of bright promises far away, star-like in a chill darkness, light still reaching his eyes from failed promises made long ago.

Grace found her coat and went outdoors. The fresh air slapped her awake. She wasn't sure what season it was. Bare branches scratching and clawing the sky, traces of snow laced with dog poop — that made it early spring. At the bus terminal on Bay Street, she asked for a schedule. Sitting down to read it, she felt dizzy. *I have nothing inside myself*, she thought. *Only Nora. That dream. What I let her do.*

She wondered if her life was over.

* * *

Grace decided to take a cab home. Feverish, she went to bed, slept and awakened and slept. Life, she thought, was a slow-acting poison. *Must be what I'm sick with.*

Three days later, she got up and began to prepare for her trip to an unknown place.

25

A WEEK AFTER NORA'S DEATH, Claire called Grace to tell her that the *Star* was running her feature the next day. Getting no answer, she drove to Grace's apartment after work. Her door was unlocked, no one home, the cupboard ajar where Grace had kept her paintings. *Shit, I forgot, she's out of town. She emailed me.* Even so, the open door troubled her. *Dumb. It's almost asking to be broken into.* The place looked emptied, as if Grace had moved out and left the key for the next occupant. Claire felt afraid, as if her friend might never come back, might never make it to her father's.

She stepped inside and peered into the cupboard, seeing Alastair's almost-finished portrait of young Todd Miller. She could feel the hurt in his affronted eyes, their endless accusation. *Guilty*, they said.

Who is? she thought. *And of what?*

Grace wouldn't abandon this painting. It seemed like a message, a lost child trapped in rage. *Seeing her dad might help*, she thought. Yet she felt uneasy.

She noticed an envelope on the floor, something Grace must have dropped. Claire picked it up. It was sealed, without an address or stamp. Inside she could feel an object, a small, hard, circular thing. She ripped it open.

Alison Lange's gold ring. A note said *This belongs to you, Dad.*

No, it does not, Claire thought. *This was given to me. You stole it, Gracie. You rifled my jewellery box and I never even noticed. It's time you damn well grew up.* She fingered it, knowing as a wife that every such ring is a circle closed by a vow. When Alastair gave it to her, he said, *You'll get over me, please God. Life's for getting over.* She'd vowed to prove him wrong. Now she recalled the depth of his love and the warmth of his arms around her. Pensive, she sensed the mystery of his kindly presence in her life.

All of this she'd gotten over. Yes.

Poor Alastair was right.

Guilty, said Todd's eyes.

The beach painting had come back to her, the gift Alastair was willing to make of what little he had. She took the ring and held it, feeling in its slight form the endless circle of lost generations and forgotten hopes. He'd carried inside of him the chill hardness of the boreal forest, more pain than anyone could bear. She remembered his unheeded books and the eerie light of his paintings. More sorrowful than either of these was the friendship she'd hungered for, the price that Alastair had paid for it.

What grave things their dreams had been. She kissed the ring. *No, Grace. This is mine.*

26

GRACE FINISHES HER CIGARETTE and goes into the bus terminal on Bay Street. She's sober, her hair done up in a knot, as well-dressed as she'll ever be in a tweed pantsuit scavenged from the Sally Ann. She travels with a backpack, like a hiker. Yet she hasn't felt her best since that rough night in the underpass a few weeks back. Nausea, dizziness. *I'm just stressed out.*

After years of exile, she's made up her mind to visit her dad because she wants to give him the joy of seeing her. She'd phoned him, asking if he were free for a visit on the dates she'd planned. To his surprise, she'd given him the details of when and where the bus would arrive. He'd pick her up, he said, and she could sense how happy he was. Yet she knows he may not be happy when she asks his forgiveness for having hidden his painting of Todd, for causing him so much suffering. Even so, he hasn't all that much longer to live, and at the rate she's going, neither has she. Knowing that she loves him, Grace also knows that she won't have forever to prove it.

She buys her ticket, waits in the terminal for the boarding announcement, then lines up for the bus, finding herself a seat next to the window. Drifting into reverie, she realizes that all her life her father's tried to give her kindness, but she hasn't paid attention. She recalls him putting a crayon in her hand and teaching her to write her name. She remembers how she'd sit with him when he'd paint, the colours pouring into her so that even now she can almost drink their brilliance. Her thoughts meander into dreams, into the radiant newness of the world spread wide, fanning out before her like the segments of an orange. A child again, she tastes the sweet moment before everything was lost.

She's four, Todd's two. Grace puts her arms around him, and she can smell the milky sweetness of his flesh. Her fingers stroke his cheek — how soft it is. *Good baby,* and her fingertips wonder if she was this soft once, with the same warm hum of life in her skin. Looking around her, she sees the room shimmering as daylight opens the windows and runs down the walls like a tiger's golden stripes. Her hand reaches out to it, resting on the sun in Todd's hair. It's warm, his hair, as if lit from within. She strokes it. *Be gentle,* says Mrs. Miller. Grace feels the petal-lightness of her own hand on his head. Later Todd falls asleep in her lap. Grace smoothes his hair, a dazzle in her fingertips, her body falling into the bright, bright sun.

Gold, she thinks, startled awake. She feels in her pocket for the envelope. *It's gone.* She must have lost it in the terminal.

It wasn't hers to keep. What is?

The bus is rolling down the highway now, and the motion makes her dizzy. Startled, she sees there's no roof above her head. She's air, no more than a warm current lifting the wings of birds, and she can sense that nothing abides, not even pain. Grandmother Alison's dead and Grandfather Tom; Lyle Miller and Nora. Her father Alastair holds her dear and he will forgive her and he will die and she will die and their story will drift into the wind.

It's over. She feels this as she lifts her hands to the sky, sees a terrible flash, its light revealing the fine tracery of a hidden world in the delicate bones of her fingers: archways, bridges, cathedrals, a dazzling city. She's innocent again on a hot summer day — floating through the dusty green of Linden, a garden sprinkler, she and Todd dancing inside the spray of mist where her father's eyes beheld them on the other side of time.

They still do.

Of all things lost, this remains with him. Safe, beloved.

Todd! she yells, and she runs with him, into the light.

Then disappears.

Acknowledgements

I would like to thank Luciana Ricciutelli and Inanna Publications for their generous support and encouragement of my work.

Thanks also to the Ontario Arts Council for allowing me creative time and means to write.

A big thank you to Irene Guilford, whose astute reading and insight has added much to this story.

And as always, thank you, Brian, first reader and a dreamer's friend.

Photo: Brian Gibson

Born and raised in the New York City area, Carole Giangrande now resides in Toronto. She is the author of the novellas *Midsummer* and *A Gardener On The Moon*, which was a co-winner of the 2010 Ken Klonsky Novella Contest. She is also the author of two novels, *An Ordinary Star* (2004) and *A Forest Burning* (2000) and a short story collection, *Missing Persons* (1994), as well as two non-fiction books: *Down To Earth: The Crisis in Canadian Farming* (1985) and *The Nuclear North: The People, The Regions and the Arms Race* (1983). She's worked as a broadcast journalist for CBC Radio, and her fiction, articles and reviews have appeared in literary journals and in Canada's major newspapers. While revising new work, she now comments as The Thoughtful Blogger (a space for interesting books and intermittent reflection), available through her website at http://www.carolegiangrande.com.